WHEN THE WORLD
ENDS

a novella by

J.L. FORREST

inspired by music from

KING MAKIS

AWAKEFM

NICEFM

"When the World Ends"

When the World Ends was written, with permission, in artistic response to the song "When the World Ends" by King Makis and AwakeFM. Neither J.L. Forrest nor Robot Cowgirl Ltd. claim any rights to the song "When the World Ends", nor do they release any rights with regard to the novella *When the World Ends,* except insofar as all parties, including NiceFM, have agreed to cross-promotion.

First Edition. Paperback. Published by the Robot Cowgirl Press:

http://robotcowgirl.com.

Design by Forstå.

Library of Congress Cataloging-in-Publication Data has been applied for.

ISBN 978-0-9989492-9-1

FURTHER READING [AND LISTENING]

Read more of J.L. Forrest—

REQUIES DAWN

DELICATE MINISTRATIONS

MINISCULE TRUTHS

Join J.L. Forrest's mailing list—

http://jlforrest.com/newsletter/

Visit J.L. Forrest's website—

http://jlforrest.com

Listen to "When the World Ends", the track which inspired this novella, and learn more about its creators at—

https://nicefm.bandcamp.com/album/when-the-world-ends-deluxe-single-novella

NiceFM

song by

King Makis and AwakeFM

Thanks to—

NiceFM

King Makis

AwakeFM

James

Johine

Mike

and as always

Shana

FOREWORD

On 18 July, 2018, the mysterious NiceFM collective messaged me, via Twitter, without so much as an e-introduction. They asked whether I'd consider writing a short story to complement a new track by music maestros AwakeFM and King Makis. After giving it a listen, and considering the overwhelming writing deadlines already on my shoulders, naturally I told them I'd do it—something brief, maybe 1,500 to 3,000 words.

They called that track "When the World Ends".

To explain the writing of this story, I need to pontificate about babies and kidney stones.

I've had more than half a dozen stones, two which required surgery, all between 2008 and 2015. During this high-pressure period, I served as Director of Study Abroad for an academic program at the University of Colorado Boulder, as well as chairing that program's Curriculum Committee.

Collegiate politics. Lies. John le Carré levels of deceit. *Stress.*

Like the *Blight* which appears in this story, job stress can kill you. During each bout with kidney stones, the initial treatment required copious morphine—or medications which performed similarly. I remember one doctor saying, "We can't give him more—he isn't taking enough breaths," and my blood oxygen kept crashing. During the worst incident, I passed out in the passenger seat of the car while my wife sped down the highway, twenty-five miles to the hospital. At one point, she feared I'd died.

The point is this: When the (often female) doctors told us that kidney stones can cause more pain than childbirth, I believed them.

Thus when I say that writing the narrative version of *When the World Ends* was like childbirth, I feel as if I've got some authority in that subject. Furthermore, the experience was like birthing triplets.

In attempt one, I conjured a Vatican-bred, far-future Catholic assassin. She'll appear in some future story.

In attempt two, I wove a twenty-second-century retelling of *Romeo and Juliet,* in which the world of the lovers comes to an abrupt end—as it did in Shakespeare's original—even if the rest of the world lives on.

In attempt three, the magic happened, and I overshot the short story by 19,000 words. Here we have it, an unexpected novella. Some of its imagery comes from my experiences, and impressions, of electronica. Throughout my life, this includes vague childhood memories in the deserts (the Wastes?) of New Mexico, when my grandmother would listen to LPs of Vangelis, Jean Michel Jarre's *Oxygène,* or Tangerine Dream. On hi-fi, of course. My later relationships with the Communikey Festival in Boulder or Seattle's Decibel Festival further colored *When the World Ends,* and I've included a particular shoutout to Rafael Irisarri, whose dreamlike soundscapes have accompanied me across many a cross-country road trip.

Here you have it: *When the World Ends.*

With many thanks to NiceFM, AwakeFM, and King Makis, I hope you enjoy this darkly tale.

J.L. Forrest
Denver, Colorado
August 2018

I. THE OLD MAN WE KILLED

Day 131—

I'VE BEEN THINKING ABOUT the old man we killed in Edmonton.

Also about how barbaric it's become, this new Dark Ages. The end is nigh, as they say, but before then all that'll be left is superstition and human sacrifices.

The ruins of Edmonton felt unreal, like a studio set for a World War immersive. Half the city burnt to foundations, some still smoking. Gangs had carved off territory, annihilating any semblance of government. But there weren't enough people left alive to have emptied Edmonton's pharmacies, and the pharmacies were worth a risk.

Antibiotics, painkillers, first-aid kits, plenty of tampons, cotton swabs.

The old man was hungry. Would've given the crazy asshole a share of venison, but he came at me, no warning. Surprised the shit out of us.

Raymond shot him, took the piss right out of him.

I sat with the grizzled moron, held his hand while he bled out. He told me about his wife, Martha, dead from Blight. He loved that woman, wouldn't talk about much except her hair and her wedding dress, how they'd had forty years together.

That was something. Do any of us have forty years anymore?

Looters had robbed his house. After that, another group adopted him, but they died. He was scared, figured

Raymond and I were killers, thought maybe he could take us before we noticed him.

Guess he was right about us being killers.

Ray's bullet ripped through his liver. Such a bad end.

I used our morphine on him, but before he went under I forgot to ask his name. Wish I could say this guy was our first kill, but Ray and I have dropped a few between Winnipeg and here. Wish I could say it was exhausting, that I was sad, that I cared.

Most of us left, that's one thing we've got in common—numbness.

In the abstract I suppose I care, but the crying is impossible.

Truth is I don't think we'll make it four years, never mind forty. I don't mean me and Raymond. I mean *Homo sapiens.*

It's been one thing after another—the Pulses, wars, Blight, all the dog-eat-dog bullshit. I keep wondering what's next, what form the killing blow will take. At this rate, a planet-destroying asteroid wouldn't surprise me.

Might be a relief to see it hit.

Ray and I are nearing Hinton, following railroad tracks, having learned our lesson about highways back in Indian Head. I miss Phil and Terry, miss the way they smiled even after everything fell apart. I figure their killers are still ripping up and down the Trans-Canada Highway, and I fantasize about finding those gang-banging assholes, chaining them behind their El Camino, and dragging them until their bones fall apart.

Only fantasy—we'll never go east again.

Hinton.

By the maps, the town wasn't that large before Blight, maybe ten thousand people. We'll chance it. Stock up on whatever we can find, then keep west until we reach Prince George.

II. HINTON

Day 132—

Two old farmers in Hinton. They sat playing cards and drinking beer. Cold cans.

Enough battery power to last a few months, they said, and they were rigging solar panels taken off houses. As far as they knew, no one else was left anywhere in Town.

Only a few hundred survived Blight, they said, and those trickled off east, most to Toronto.

We passed no one heading east, we told them. East is dead.

"We heard the government was pulling things together in Toronto," said the farmers.

Ray asked if they heard that on a radio.

No. Nothing on a radio, only what a few passersby were saying. Meaning Toronto was dark.

Could be a post-apocalyptic utopia in the making. Probably it's hell.

Not more than a quarter million Torontonians survived Blight. Half those have died since. Last news was of cholera out-breaks, for fuck's sake. Whatever you do, don't go to Toronto.

The farmers shuffled the cards. We drank beer together and played a few hands.

On our way out of town, Raymond and I passed mass graves. In the fields north of the tracks, two bulldozers sat idle beside the mounds, grass crowding the treads. Ash darkened the clay.

In Winnipeg they burned the bodies, torched them as fast as they could. Probably wise, stopped a lot of disease.

Not Blight, though.
It killed everyone it touched.

> Jimmy
> Connie
> Aaron
> Tim
> Sidhu
> Bethany
> Ed
> Cee
> Mom
> Dad

The Pulses sure messed up the world, but Blight put the human race down. A hammer between the eyes. A knife to the intestines.

Sometimes, I think anyone who died of Blight got the better deal. But I'm still alive, I still want to live, and if I haven't given up by now, I'm not going to.

By tomorrow, we'll be in the mountains.

III. MCBRIDE

DAY 148—

THE TRACKS LED US through Jasper, then for two and half days the rails followed the Fraser River and Robson Valley. This afternoon we reached McBride.

If anyone here survived Blight, they're long gone, which could mean either walked away or dead from something else.

In the fields, I estimate two hundred marked graves. We guess as many corpses in town. There is a convenience to apocalypses, I suppose, the way people find religion again, the way they pack themselves into churches to die. Half the dead are in the local church, the stink faded, and we steered wide of it.

Now I sit on the porch of a white farmhouse on a cool evening. The summer's getting late. I've been counting days but I can't tell you the date or day of week. It's August, I'm sure.

Hints of wood smoke on the air.

Across the world, fires have gotten worse for decades. Higher temperatures. Longer summers. Less rain in some places, more in others, where the grasses grow taller and burn easier. Today, there might be a hundred wildfires across Canada. Fewer humans to start them, but no one to put them out. Forests surround this ghost town, hug the rail lines through these mountains, many trees still living but way too many dead and dry.

God, I hope I don't die in a fire.

Raymond managed to light the house's gas stove. Warm beans, canned spinach, spaghetti and meatballs—

canned food for dinner. We've walked most of the way from Winnipeg, and this was one of the best meals I've ever eaten.

He wants to go upstairs and fuck, like a regular couple, in a bed.

That sounds pretty grand.

Wait. Shit. There are lights moving at the edge of town—

↓

↓

↓

↓

It was a party going east. We warned them about Toronto, but they're heading across Banff, want to make it across Alberta. They warned us not to go north of Prince George, said we were all but dead if we did.

Something about the "Horned Lords." Whatever the hell.

Monsters in the Yukon. Cannibals, they said. Crazy, they said.

That's a real problem, seeing as our destination is Fairbanks.

Ray has brought back gallons of water. He's boiling pot-fuls, carrying them upstairs to the bathtub. Not like we have to conserve the propane. When the water cools enough, we can take a bath.

A bath!

Good man.

He is absolutely getting laid tonight.

IV. CONVERSATIONS

CONVERSATION—

TRYING TO REMEMBER CONVERSATIONS. I don't want all our words lost. Someone should record what people said, what we thought, why we argued what we argued.

RAY:	Cannibals don't sound so good.
ME:	You mean, like, for dinner?
RAY:	Gross.
ME:	See what I did there?
RAY:	You know what I meant.
ME:	Yeah. Cannibals sound fucking terrifying.
RAY:	So maybe we don't go up Highway 16?
ME:	Ya think? Cannibals, Ray.
RAY:	What if we go west, to the coast?
ME:	And do what?
RAY:	There must be heaps of abandoned boats.
ME:	What'll we do with a boat?
RAY:	Take it up the coast?
ME:	To where?
RAY:	Anchorage.
ME:	Anchorage is drowned.
RAY:	Yeah, but there was news of reconstruction there. Anchorage was coming back.
ME:	That was before Blight.
RAY:	Worth a try. Even if Anchorage is dead, there'd be routes to Fairbanks from there.
ME:	Only one problem with that plan.

RAY:	Which is?
ME:	Neither of us knows how to sail.
RAY:	What if it's a motorboat?
ME:	That's open water. On the ocean. And what about fuel?
RAY:	We stay close to land?
ME:	Rocks?
RAY:	I begin to see your point.
ME:	Still, drowning in seawater or being dashed on rocks sound better than cannibals.
RAY:	What if a storm took us way out to sea and we got lost?
ME:	Then I suppose we'd starve to death.
RAY:	I'd sacrifice myself so you could eat.
ME:	Gross.
RAY:	See what I did there? I suppose you'd still die of thirst.
ME:	Ya think?

Then the sonic boom ripped across the sky.

A low-altitude StratoJumper. They hit Mach 9, and "low altitude" means fifty thousand feet on their way up to one twenty, enough to hang with a hook, transfer passengers or goods to orbit, then glide to the ground.

This has always been true:

The ultra-rich patronize us, tell us the problems of the poor are exactly like their problems, only less so, that money doesn't make anyone happier. Money makes the problems bigger, they explain. Money is only for the strong and capable, they argue. Great wealth is a sign of character and moral backbone, they claim. At the same time their commercials sell us the jet-setter lifestyle, guilt us for not having it. At the same time they tell us to live within our means. Climb the ladder. Improve our station. Work hard enough or smart enough, and you too can be a bazillionaire.

Before Blight, were ten billion of us too lazy or stupid to measure up? Do dollars make morals?

I glimpsed the StratoJumper, half a sky ahead of its engines' growl. No one on that ship is worried about starving tonight. Or about breaking a leg and dying in the sticks. Or about highway bandits, rapists, or murderers.

If the rumours of cannibals in the north are true, well, I wish they'd follow their Rousseau: "When the people shall have nothing more to eat," he said, "they will eat the rich."

I might try a bite or two myself.

V. PULSE, PARTS I & II

PULSES ONE AND TWO—

SUPPOSEDLY THERE'S STILL ICE on Greenland, but most is already gone, went in earnest. At their most rapid, Long Island-sized chunks were dropping into the ocean every hour, week after week, month after month. In a geological sense, million-year-old ice vanished like underwear on a virgin's wedding night. By then, Arctic permafrost had turned into swamp. Canada, Russia, Sweden, Norway, and Finland belched their stores of methane.

"You started this fight," said the Earth. "Now, you little morons, I'm gonna finish it."

Within a few months, coastal waterlines rose six meters. The first cities drowned. Italy wasn't a quarter done with its sea walls—too much corruption to complete the job—and arrivederci Venice. Manhattan got its feet wet. People fled Miami. I remember none of this—I was a toddler.

While I was in kindergarten, Antarctica's entire ring of sea ice calved, floated away, and melted, but that didn't impact sea levels. If you don't believe me, and you're still lucky enough to have refrigeration, watch the ice cubes melt into your next glass of water.

But that ring was holding back a few epochs' worth of landlocked ice. "It'll take a thousand years to melt," said the optimists.

In unison the ice melted top and bottom. Beneath the glaciers, water provided lubrication, and Antarctican bedrock isn't flat. The first true slide happened over the course of three years. I was thirteen when more Long Islands drop, drop, dropped into the South Pacific. To image what this does, fill your water glass to the top, then drop the ice cubes in.

Pulse Two.

During my first year of high school, coastlines jumped seventeen meters.

Halifax and Montréal treaded water. Boston, New York, Philadelphia, D.C., and all the Eastern Seaboard cities became the New Venices. Vancouver, Seattle, and Portland took a splash. Huge disasters in India. Croplands lost in China. Water wars in Africa and the Middle East. Southeast Asia suffered from below and above—inundation along with perennial, unending rainfalls. In the United States, California dried up while Cascadia traded drizzles for downpours.

VI. VISIONS, PART I

DAY 153—

I HAD A DREAM. Craziest in a long time, and today I can't quite shake it.

We're halfway between McBride and Prince George. Last night, we slept a ways off the tracks, up in the pines. The perfume of forest fires keeps teasing our nostrils but, after dark, no orange tinges any horizon. The trees here are full and green, unlike the dead stands in the foothills west of Edmonton.

Before bedding down, we spotted a flashlight on the other side of the valley, someone walking the far line of trees. We've learned not to go chasing after people. Half the time that goes terribly.

I've been thinking about the two boys we killed in Saskatoon.

Anyway, the dream.

At night it's been warm enough that we haven't needed a fire, though autumn's coming. Raymond and I only smoke meat while the sun shines, and we don't burn wood outside daylight hours—too easy to attract the wrong kinds of attention.

I've been thinking about the woman I had to shoot before we got to Lloydminster.

In my dream, Ray and I are sleeping beside a cozy fire. He's got his arms around me. I wake up—not actually wake up, but in the dream I'm awake—and a woman is crouching on the other side of the fire pit. Her pale irises drink me in. Kohl rims her eyes, and her loose, azure clothes cover everything but her face and hands. Her long, delicate, alabaster fingers trace strange, intricate patterns in the air.

Behind her, in the darkness, animals circle the fire. Their eyes reflect the light.

"You're Bettina," she says to me.

"You're Cailín," I say, having no doubt as to her name.

She moves around the fire, taking my earthy hands in hers, and she kisses me. Luscious kiss. Awake, Raymond reclines and watches us, neither sophomorically amused nor selfishly detached, his gaze both warm and preternaturally dark. He observes us as he might savor a beautiful sunrise or a breathtaking thunderstorm.

Only after Cailín reduces me to a quivering, moaning mess does Ray join us. Limbs and mouths, everything soft and hard, breathy and desperate.

That's how I knew it was a dream. The sex was too, too excellent.

Cailín.

Why would I remember a name from a dream?

VII. PULSE, PART III

Pulse Three—

After Pulses One and Two, we the ninety-nine percent learned how rich the one percent always were. The Corkscrews went up, literal magic-rope tricks into space. They built new orbital stations, nice ones, not like the ISS but more like luxury resorts. Funded from China, Europe, America, Japan.

Funded by governments. Funded privately. No difference.

Not funded for the masses.

Anyone with a telescope could watch the launches, the orbiters, the space elevators. Anyone with a car could drive to the ground facilities, to the cordoned gates, to the guards with their machine guns. Anyone with a brain could predict this future.

Nonetheless, most of Canada, the U.S., and Europe pretended like everything would someday return to "situation normal." England kept calm and carried on while the ocean marched up the Thames.

I graduated. I went to a great college.

To this day, I cannot tell you

the point of college.

Not quite true.

I can.

At least my mother had the sense to realize there was no purpose in business administration, accounting, or law. Wasn't like little me could do a damn thing to save the world, so I studied whatever I wanted. I studied art, history, philosophy, literature, poetry, and music—those were the points. I majored in English and minored in gender studies. I partied.

Fuck the patriarchy.

Sometimes the patriarchy fucked me, or its sons did. Mustn't get pregnant—I've always been careful with the birth control!

Only a monster would bring children into this world.

The next catastrophic glacial calvings came five years ago, right after postgrad. Pulse Three, bigger than One and Two combined.

Thirty-three meters, all by itself. If I wrote the names of the sunken cities, I'd run out of pencils, and it could be a while before I find another box. Florida and most of the U.S. Gulf Coast submerged—a true Atlantis—the irony of the Southern oil industry and that drill, baby, drill bullshit.

A Second Great Depression, they called it. Markets tumbled, avalanches of money dropping into bottomless pits. Two hundred trillion dollars evaporated. Economies in tatters.

How stupid. Rats shredding each other as the bilges filled.

Canada went bankrupt, my alma mater closed, and my diploma isn't worth shit.

VIII. PRINCE GEORGE

DAY 158—

PRINCE GEORGE IS THE closest I've seen to civilization since quitting Winnipeg. Compared to Edmonton's anti-civilization, killing-in-the-streets, Hobbesian state of nature, Prince George shines, a beacon of possibilities. Before Blight, Prince George's population pushed ninety thousand. Now it's twenty thousand, but that's equal to Edmonton, and Prince Georgians cohabit well. Like us, most came from somewhere else.

Walls surround the city. In places they're flimsy, but workers orbit them like satellites, reinforcing them at each pass. Corrugated steel replaces fencing. Concrete reinforces the steel. Battlements emerge from the concrete.

At the eastern gates, guardsmen searched us, made us relinquish our guns. They locked them into strongboxes.

"This system doesn't work if all we do is hoard guns," they told us.

"You'll get them back," they told us.

Prince George operates under a benevolent monarchy. The man calls himself—drumroll—Prince George.

Marshals patrol the streets. They maintain a bartering market, which they tax. The city sponsors workshops—blacksmiths, leatherworkers, mechanics, carpenters, computer repair. Solar panels cover every roof, and Prince George stockpiles batteries. Its militarized teams harvest household power supplies from every building within a hundred klicks.

Once we got our bearings, understood how the settlement functioned, we traded most of our venison for a few nights in the hotel. Second hot bath in a fortnight! A room with a lock on the door!

The barroom served beer and it doubled as a newsroom. These days, satellite and dirigible internet were intermittent, and anyway Russian hackers had rewritten billions of websites with Cyrillic garbage. Television dead. Radio unreliable.

At the bar, everyone talked with everyone else, one part gossip blender, one part information network. We met a group we like—Robert, Faith, Garret, and Sadzie—who shared their experiences freely. Sadzie is descended from the Deg Hit'an, knows a few words of the language, maybe one of the last in the world who do. A weight hangs about her, like instead of her walking upon the land, the land rides on her shoulders.

Robert and Faith make me think Ken and Barbie, ridiculously caucasian, nauseatingly WASPy, but they strike me as earnest and goodhearted. Faith wears a gaudy cross on an oversized chain around her neck. Garret is shorter than I am, a mess of curly hair, a dark beard, and a paunch. In forty years, he'd be Santa Claus.

Our conversation turned serious.

SADZIE:	You cannot go north.
RAY:	Why?
SADZIE:	If you do, you'll die.
RAY:	What's up there? We've heard stories of cannibals.
SADZIE:	They call themselves the Horned Lords.
RAY:	Who are they?
SADZIE:	Men who welcome monsters into their hearts, who have become monsters, who aren't men anymore.

RAY:	What does that mean?
ROBERT:	Means serious shit, that's what.
FAITH:	We came south from Whitehorse. Lost friends along the way.
ROBERT:	What she means is the Horned Lords murdered them.
ME:	A lot of people killing other people out there. Violence is everywhere.
ROBERT:	Not like this.
RAY:	What do you mean?
ROBERT:	Skinning people alive. Disemboweling them, then keeping them from death. Burning them millimeters at a time. Feeding them to ants—
FAITH:	Jesus, Robert, that's enough.
ROBERT:	They need to know.
SADZIE:	The world is emptying, making room for spirits again. Raven is out and about.
ME:	Raven?
SADZIE:	The Trickster.
FAITH:	Jesus—
GARRET:	Here's the point—unless you want to die, screaming and spitting up your own innards, don't cross north of the Skeena River. There are scary motherfuckers up there, and they seem to be everywhere at once. I tend to agree with Sadzie—we may live in a world of communicable superbugs, climate change, economics, spaceships, and technological wonders, but what I saw up north, that was some serious supernatural shit. Don't go

anywhere near it. Before Blight, I was CTO for a ten-billion-dollar company. Google was looking at acquiring us. I'm no woo-woo superstitious idiot, but I know what I saw up there, and it scared the crap out of me.

RAY: We hear the U.S. military is taking refugees in Fairbanks, that it's far enough north they're setting up giant farming operations, a walled city, infrastructure.

ROBERT: We hear that too, but you'll never get there from here.

RAY: What about heading out the Yellowhead Highway to the coast? Taking a boat to Alaska?

ROBERT: Maybe, but there're pirates up and down the Haida Gwaii.

RAY: Pirates? As in arrrrrrh?

ROBERT: Forced boardings, looting, murdering, raping, scuttling. Yeah, arrrrrrh.

RAY: Where are you going then?

FAITH: South.

RAY: South is death. South is drought, fire, war.

GARRET: There's a Corkscrew in San Francisco.

ME: Corkscrew? As in stairway to heaven? I thought San Francisco was drowned?

GARRET: Not entirely. The trillionaire Avidità built a space elevator and he's taking thousands up every day—people like us, not über-one-percenters.

RAY: Thought you said you were a CTO?
              Isn't that a one-percenter?
GARRET: I said Google was looking at acquiring
              us, not that they did. Anywho, Avidità
              has got two Stations in orbit—genera-
              tion ships.
ME: Big?
GARRET: Enough to preserve entire ecosystems,
              wait things out a millennium or two.
              Why don't you come with us?

Color me gobsmacked. Hobgoblins and space stations,
all in one day.

IX. BLIGHT

BLIGHT—

WHEN SORROWS COME, THEY come not single spies, but in battalions.

Global, world-quaking battalions.

Warming, droughts, famines.

Economic collapse.

Rising waters.

Fires.

We thought we had it bad, but the ten billion of us figured we'd have another generation or ten to work it out. This wasn't like dinosaurs and a collision with a gigantic space rock. Did you know most of the dinosaurs were dead within a year?

Climate change would take time to kill ten billion.

Blight changed that.

Blight, definition: a plant disease, typically one caused by fungi such as mildews, rusts, and smuts; a thing which spoils or damages something.

Noticeable symptoms of Blight begin in the lungs with a dry, unproductive cough, chest pain, wheezing, and shortness of breath. Irritation of the throat, nose, eyes, and ears follows. From first cough to varying degrees of blindness and deafness takes seven to nine days.

Yellow, flaky mushrooms grow from the skin, and victims shed their hair. After another week, the skin resembles paperbark.

Dementia-like symptoms follow, including disorientation, memory loss, and delusions. Near the end, the afflicted lose language, muscle control, and intestinal functions. They babble, cough, and shit themselves to death.

As near as we can figure, the infection rate was ninety-eight percent.

The fatality rate, one hundred.

Ten months passed from the disease's first appearance in Myanmar to the last time I saw anyone still living with it, in Portage la Prairie. Give or take, nine billion eight hundred million people died in less than a year.

What's wilder, though, is I can't shake this feeling that the Earth isn't done doling out the sorrows, that the Earth means to beat us down till we stay down. When you've taken enough of a beating, when the blows fall enough times, you expect them to keep coming. My PTSD has PTSD, and I know it's not over.

Blight killed everyone I loved. What could be worse than Blight?

I don't know, but I wish whatever it is would get on with it.

X. THE HORNED LORDS

Day 160—

THE HORRORS OF THIS day will remain with me the rest of my life, but when I remember them, I want to remember them right. I owe this to—to the dead? To some unlikely posterity? To myself?

What if all I'm doing is recording the days before the world ends? Every time I write, I ask this question, and every time I keep writing.

Early this morning, Raymond and I fought. I wish we hadn't, not today.

But we did, screamed in one another's face. We weren't fighting each other, not really, though we stomped and yelled and called each other names. We were fighting our self-doubts, our second-guessing, our emotional exhaustion. I'm sure our neighbors in the hotel appreciated our shrieking, our roaring at each other like those extinct dinosaurs.

I've been thinking about all those species erased in the Cretaceous.

Tiny mammals survived, of course, and a few of those dinosaurs did too. They became birds.

Maybe we can become birds?

Because we were hungry, Ray and I finally gave up fighting. A nearby diner served us eggs, turkey sausage, asparagus, pancakes, and maple syrup.

A world with maple syrup can't be so bad, can it?

Over breakfast, once more, we reviewed our options. North to be tortured and eaten by woo-woo cannibals. West to be raped and murdered by pirates. East the way we came, the Great Plains of nothing and no one. South into the wastelands to chase down a magic rope-trick elevator into the Shangri-La sky, built by some eccentric gazillionaire, which sounded far too good to be true.

ME: Those all suck, but you're right—west
                is by far our best choice, then into the
                Alaska interior.

RAY: Glad you see it that way. Listen, Bett,
                I've seen notices in town. There're whole
                groups going west, maybe a hundred
                people, aiming to make it into the U.S.
                Army's cordon zone. Pirates can't kill
                a hundred of us, can they? We stick
                together and we'll be fine.

ME: I trust you, Ray.

RAY: All right. Let's get everything together.
                We can hit the trail before dark.

Before we left the diner, we kissed.

Prince George extends no farther west than what used to be the Cariboo Highway, bounded on that side by a meter-thick, four-meter high concrete-and-steel wall. Beyond the wall extend the dissolving ruins of abandoned suburbs. A gate faces the Nechako River bridge, and steel fencing lines either side of Fifth. The fencing squeezes new arrivals, funnels them, into what used to be a schoolyard. Funnel and schoolyard are killing grounds, and these define the city's true edge, a buffer between the outer wall and central district. Textbook defensive structure of a typical medieval town.

Safety first.

When the shit came down, Ray and I found ourselves, at least, on the correct side of the fence. Panic arose from the walls and gate. The doors opened but, from where we stood, what flowed through them resembled a clown parade, some creation of conceptual performance art. Shuffling figures—

I remembered every zombie flick I'd ever seen—

No, this was something else.

We rushed to the fencing, the chain-link around the schoolyard, as shouts crescendoed from the town's northwest boundary. Cries of OH GOD, OH GOD reached our ears.

Prince George's marshals rallied, sprinting by with rifles or machine guns. Snipers hurried along the tops of the walls, taking aim at this clown-troop horror which bumbled past the gates.

Hobbled.

Limped.

Staggered.

Forty meters from me, thirty, twenty. A few dozen people (could I call them people?) dragged their feet, feeling with their toes, testing the street before each step. Four sheepdogs circled their periphery, herding what used to be (what were still?) men and women. They emptied into the schoolyard, where they could progress no farther, and the dogs packed them into a tight mob, nipping their heels, driving them against each other. One fell but struggled back to its feet.

I call it an it because I couldn't discern he or she or they in any gendered sense.

Their naked bodies painted black, altogether these dozens resembled quivering shadows. Armless, each of them, limbs severed at the shoulders. They mewed, lowing like cattle, and while their heads turned this way and that, they fixated on nothing. Their eyes shown no brighter than the rest of their faces—meaning they shone not at all—and as they pressed to the fence, I backed away.

I must have screamed.

Their eyelids sewn shut, the flesh beneath their brows shrank into their skulls. Their ears, too, folded forward, sewn closed. A black, shiny, pasty substance coated their skin.

Its scent, familiar.

Two Horned Lords followed them. Burly men wearing wild leathers, their faces smeared in red clay, their long beards in blue-dyed braids. Violet, liquid lines dripped from the corners of their mouths. Caribou antlers extended from their skulls.

Headdresses, I realized, not some novel species. Only men.

From the battlements, the snipers aimed into the mob, aimed at the Horned Lords, aimed at the barking dogs.

A woman trailed the Lords. A long cord tied her wrists, and another stretched between her ankles—she could walk but not run. Like the Lords, she wore deerskin or elk hide, hers bleached white. Her dark plaits hung to her waist and Kohl rimmed her eyes.

She looked right at me.

I would write that my knees turned to water, but one should be careful with metaphors in worlds with magic. Similes could become realities.

I knew her, of course, at once recalled her name.

Cailín.

As she held my gaze, the world remade itself in silence, as if God had crafted it from dead brick, as if God had shut my ears too. Only slowly did I realize a Horned Lord was speaking, his voice booming across the schoolyard, rising to the walls, reaching into the city's heart. He wasn't shouting, no. He could have been whispering, but his every word travelled everywhere, as if to every onlooker at once.

LORD I: Red for power! Blue for order! White for mourning! Black for death! Remember these, Prince George—

LORD II: Prince George, you needn't fear. Prince George, the Elder Gods have returned to us, will carry us into our future, will set right all things which man has ruined. Rejoice! The Earth will not die, but live on. Prince George, all you must do is renounce everything you believe, pledge everything you are to the Gods, and accompany us. Prince George, do this and nothing will ever again frighten you, nothing will ever hurt you, nothing will ever stand between you and Paradise on Earth.

LORD I: Resist us, deny the Elder Gods, and—

This first Lord gestured to the tongueless, eyeless, earless, armless herd. No one misunderstood his meaning. He clapped twice, and every one of the herd dropped to their knees. The dogs retreated and gathered behind Cailín.

RAY: Bett, we have to get the hell out of here.

From their robes the Lords drew road flares and, as if by sorcery, the flares erupted into red flame. The marshals and guards opened fire, riddling the Lords with bullets, lead tearing through leather, flesh, and bone.

Not enough, not nearly.

Before the Lords fell, those flares arced into the black-painted huddle of broken humans. Before they landed, a breeze carried a phosphorous sting to my nostrils, and I placed the scent of oil and pitch.

Flames rolled through the killing floor, the heat palpable. Standing at the fence line, the explosion kissed my face, singeing my hair and eyebrows. The pork stink of burnt hair overwhelmed me. The burning victims scattered, colliding with each other, scrambling, falling, rolling, rising again and hopping in every direction. Many crashed into the fences, rebounding from the chain link, spattering the grass with sizzling fire.

Others hit the old schoolhouse, Prince George's customs house. Fire rolled up its brick-clad sides, caressed the window frames, and licked the eaves.

The marshals shot everything which moved, and the machine guns unloaded. The Horned Lords fell, Lord One laughing as he dropped to his knees, laughing until a round cleaved his skull, throwing the antlers from his headdress. Bullets ripped through the burning men, though most had already collapsed, squirming or merely twitching. More bullets came, and more and more, ricocheting from asphalt and concrete, pinging from the customs building, which joined the conflagration. Bullets sparked from steel posts. Bullets rattled. Bullets zinged.

Ray ducked, prone, to the grass. A bullet rang by my ear, and another clipped my cheek before I regained my senses, before I could pull my gaze from Cailín, who stood on the other side of the fray, the dogs at her feet with their tails between their legs.

I lay beside Ray. The gunfire continued in bursts, petered, and finally ended. Greasy plague-black smoke roiled across the yard, through the streets, into the sky. The crackle of burning bodies overtook all other sound, undergirded by a growing roar as the northwest façade of the building succumbed.

I spoke to Ray.

I shook Ray.

I compressed Ray's chest.

I breathed into Ray's mouth.

I pushed my hands to Ray's bullet-torn side and his blood washed them.

I lay across Ray.

I cried on Ray.

I lost Ray.

I looked up, meeting Cailín's unbroken gaze. Smoke thickened between us. The marshals took custody of her and led her away.

I crouched, alone.

I wish Ray and I hadn't fought.

Not today.

XI. VISIONS, PART II

A DREAM—

RAY: Jesus, Bett, that didn't go so well, did it?

ME: I'm so sorry, Ray.

RAY: Think nothing of it. Life is short.

ME: It was a good plan you had, trying to make it to Fairbanks.

RAY: The best laid schemes o' mice an' men / Gang aft a-gley.

ME: You weren't the one with an English degree, Ray. I'm thinking this is my dream, not yours, and you're only a version of myself.

RAY: Maybe, but it was still a fine plan.

ME: It was.

RAY: Head south, Bett. Go with Robert, Faith, Garret, and Sadzie. They're good-hearted people.

ME: You think there's really a space elevator in San Francisco?

RAY: I know there is, baby. I can see it from here.

XII. PRISON BARS

Day 162—

AFTER I BURIED RAYMOND in the fields west of Prince George, I agreed to trek south with Robert's group, though it might be more accurate to say they agreed to take me in. Fifth wheel. Fifth dimension. Fifth column. Fifth to a party of four. They need to arrange vehicles, fuel, and other details, but they mean to leave tomorrow.

At noon, I wandered Prince George by myself. Once I stopped crying—I wasn't sure I could cry these days, but it turns out I can—I sorted Ray's possessions, repacked what I needed with my own gear, then bartered the rest of his trappings for dried fish, ammunition, and more tampons.

The marshals brought the Horned Lords' sheepdogs to the city kennel. One had been injured, so they shot it. A local shepherd bought two. The fourth cowered in a corner, curled up on a pad of cold concrete. I traded six Big Turk candy bars for the dog. I fed him and he decided I was his best friend.

After that, I visited the jail, on Queensway. Only one marshal guarded the cells, which held a few drunks and Cailín. The marshal let me enter the jail, though this broke all the rules, and to convince him I gave him more than I wanted.

On one side of the prison bars, I sat in a chair. On the other, Cailín rested on a cot.

The kohl had smeared from around her eyes, trailing her cheeks. Her irises were a stupidly bright blue. Her lips were dark violet.

CAILÍN:	Bettina.
ME:	How is this possible? I even know the smell of you—
CAILÍN:	The Horned Lords weren't lying about the Elder Gods, and with the Elder Gods come miracles.
ME:	You were in my dream.
CAILÍN:	Was it a dream?
ME:	Yes.
CAILÍN:	Shame, it was sexy, you're sexy.
ME:	Is your accent Scottish?
CAILÍN:	Don't be silly. Irish.
ME:	How did you get here?
CAILÍN:	Long story. When Blight hit, I was in Canada for work.
ME:	What're the marshals going to do with you?
CAILÍN:	Torture me, I expect, try to learn everything about the Horned Lords that I know, make me spill my secrets.
ME:	Why don't you tell them now?
CAILÍN:	I've already have, but they didn't believe half of it, and to be sure they'll torture me regardless.
ME:	Then what?
CAILÍN:	Hang me. Burn me? I couldn't see that end so clearly.
ME:	Did you do those horrible things to those people? Cut off their arms? Take out their eyes? All that?
CAILÍN:	Would you believe me if I said no?
ME:	Yes.

CAILÍN:	Then no.
ME:	Why did the Horned Lords tie your wrists and ankles?
CAILÍN:	Because they didn't want me to escape.
ME:	Why did they bring you along?
CAILÍN:	Because the Elder Gods give women different gifts than men, and ours are rarer.
ME:	What gifts?
CAILÍN:	The future, the past, the distant, the different. We see, hear, and speak what the men cannot.
ME:	I don't understand.

Her smile was like an Irish sunrise in July.

ME:	Honestly, I'd get you out of this if I could.
CAILÍN:	You can.
ME:	How?

She told me. Then a raven landed on the window of her cell.

No shit—she called him Nevermore.

XIII. GOING SOUTH

Day 163—

YESTERDAY, BEFORE THE MARKET closed, I traded Raymond's rifle to the town. Prince George's monarch forbids arms trading between private citizens. Only the town can trade in weapons.

The town gave me gold, and I exchanged the gold to a silversmith who gave me polished earrings, a necklace, and a shiny belt buckle. Following Cailín's instruction, I left the silver on a tree stump in Connaught Hill Park. As the sun set, I observed the stump from a park bench.

Eventually, a conspiracy of ravens, twenty at least, collected the silver and flew away.

Today, I recovered my weapons from Prince George's marshals, joined with Robert's group, and we began south on Highway 97. I wasn't the fifth wheel but the seventh. Robert had hired two heavies, Cuth and Frank, who provided three trucks, six drums of petrol, and weapons. Tall and overweight, Cuth and Frank struck me as Albertan countryside-hayseed rednecks, but they came as a package deal with the vehicles. They drank accordingly, snoring away the night before our departure.

Before dawn, I did two things—

First, I watched the ravens gather at the jailhouse.
Second, I repacked a trunk in the bed of the third truck.

It's two thousand two hundred kilometers from Prince George to San Francisco. Before the Third Pulse, we might have made the drive in two days. After it, with disintegrating road conditions and detours at Bellingham, Everett, Seattle, Kent, Tacoma, Olympia, and Portland, the trip might have taken six. After Blight, it's anyone's guess. Robert hopes we can make it in ten.

Truck one—Cuth, Faith, and Robert.

Truck two—Garret and Sadzie.

Truck three—Frank, me, and the dog.

On the way from town, as we eased onto the highway, Frank played music on his truck's sound system. The first tunes I'd heard in five months, dreamy and digital, far too polished and high tech for seven grubby survivalists on their way into to the Wastes. I'd assumed Frank would be a country-and-western guy—people can surprise you.

I told him the music was nice and asked him what it was.

"When the World Ends," he said, giving me the track title.

"Catchy," he said.

"Kind of pulls you in and won't let you go," he said, looking down the road.

Won't let you go.

I wondered if he was still talking about the song, or about this world which is chewing itself up and us along with it. I sort of wished it would chew faster, to save me from what was coming next.

XIV. PRIESTESS

DAY 165—

WE'RE LUCKY TO BE alive, but any dreams I had of safety in numbers have melted down like any no-longer-maintained uranium reactor anywhere on Earth. I had hoped my stage-magician trick would go over better, but instead it ended more like Roy Horn in the tiger's mouth.

Is this making any sense?

Let me back up.

Humans need to pee and will continue producing urine even when they're not drinking. Between urination, respiration, and perspiration, the body can lose two litres per day, more with exercise. That goes on for longer than a couple of days, and your average person is in a lot of trouble. Assuming you want to keep someone alive, this makes human trafficking more difficult than, say, smuggling cocaine.

Eventually, I had to unpack the trunk from the bed of truck three. From the start, I hadn't been able to store more than a days' water in it, not if I was going to leave room for a body, and I hadn't found anything like a catheter for trade anywhere in Prince George.

Let me back up again.

A raven brought the jail key to Cailín, while scores more distracted the guard. By the time he raised the alarm, by the time marshals would have searched the town, we were navigating the potholes of Highway 97 southbound. All seven of us, as far as six of us were concerned.

That was two days ago.

Earlier today, at the junction to the Trans-Canada Highway, besides a burnt-out town once known as Hope, Cailín and I spent twenty minutes on our knees with Frank and Cuth holding pistols to our heads. Garret shouted that they couldn't kill me, I shouted that they couldn't kill Cailín, Frank shouted that I was a lying hussy who needed to pay, Cuth shouted that Cailín was a goddamned witch who had to die, and Faith implored us all to accept Jesus into our hearts.

Robert listened quietly, which was weird, because he exudes more leader mojo than the rest put together. Sadzie sat on the wrecked-out foundation wall of a razed suburban house, smoking a cigarette, studiously ignoring us.

She looked over her shoulder only when Robert made the declaration:

"We're not killing them."

It's cold tonight. I've wrapped myself in every layer I own, and I'm still shivering. They've tied Cailín to the tree beside me and, while they've left me my pack and my hands, they've taken my guns and cinched my ankles together. Frank watches us, sitting in a foldout chair with his pistol in his lap. In a few hours, Frank will turn in, then Garret or one of the others will take watch.

The sheepdog has curled up between us, and he's warm.

Whenever Robert, Faith, Garret, Frank, or Cuth talk, they whisper. Sadzie brings us food, but she doesn't say anything.

They're still trying to decide what to do with us.

Frank has closed his eyes and he's snoring.

ME:	What's the dog's name?
CAILÍN:	He doesn't have one.
ME:	Are you a witch?

CAILÍN:	A witch is something people call uppity women they don't like.
ME:	That's one definition.
CAILÍN:	I'm a priestess.
ME:	Of?
CAILÍN:	These days I serve many Gods, but Nodens most of all.
ME:	Nodens? Who's that?
CAILÍN:	The Horned Lord.
ME:	You mean like those men you were with back in Prince George?
CAILÍN:	No, nothing like them. Nodens is not a man. Nodens is nothing like a man.
ME:	Why didn't you go back north?
CAILÍN:	You're going to California, aren't you?
ME:	I suppose so.
CAILÍN:	Then I'm going to California too. I dreamed my path, and my path is with you.
ME:	Why me?
CAILÍN:	Ask Nodens.

Frank woke up, snorted, and told us to shut up. Far above us in the night sky, a StratoJumper boomed, taking another load of rich people to orbit.

XV. FIRE IN THE SKY

Day 167—

HER TASTE IS LIKE licorice or marshmallow.

An odd, pleasant, lingering flavor.

Last night was as cold as the night before, but I was much warmer. The sheepdog slept to my right, against my sleeping bag. Cailín slept inside the bag, pressed against me, so warm that after she felt asleep I unzipped the side of the bag to cool down. Before that we had sex on the blankets, under the stars, with the forest breezes caressing our skin.

The sex felt like the most natural thing in the world. Of course we were going to have sex. We'd already had sex.

Except we hadn't.

Except we had.

Hadn't we?

In the trees around us, the ravens roosted, imbued with their own particular spook factor. Nearby slept Nevermore, biggest of them all, a bird as large as a Maine Coon. Between the dog and ravens, I figure no one can sneak up on us, which is fortunate because Robert and company absconded with my guns and ammunition, even my knife.

Assholes.

"Was all this in your visions?" I asked Cailín.

"It doesn't work that way," she answered. "I thought I would hang in Prince George."

Long before dawn, the southern sky turned orange. I woke Cailín.

ME: Fire.
CAILÍN: The wind is blowing south.
ME: It could turn on us. Shouldn't we pack
                 up camp?
CAILÍN: The land says it's going south.
ME: Okay.
CAILÍN: How happy are you right now?

I didn't know how to answer. Happy, in a sense. Ray hasn't been in the ground a week, but I knew him for less than five months, and I've cried for Ray already. Before Blight, I had parents, siblings, and lovers, all of whom I knew for years. Those tears came early and dried themselves out.

How happy are you right now?

Is that a metaphor?

She's right—the wind is northerly. If we strike out overland in the dark, we're likely as not to either run across the fire's path or blunder into some other problem.

I kiss her throat, her chin, her peculiar-tasting mouth.

Wildfires lend the southern horizon a romantic glow.

XVI. BURNT OFFERINGS

Day 170—

Would we have died too? We'll never know.

Following the railroad from Hope, we walked two days without sighting another human, though yesterday we spotted a military drone patrolling nearer the coast. It paid no attention to us.

Best we can tell from the map, north of Abbotsford we'll have to cut across overgrown farmland. From there, rails cross the completely inconsequential U.S. border.

Build a wall, they once said.

Stop immigration, they once said.

Nearing the former United States, we entered the gravitational pull of Vancouver's ruins, and the abandoned vehicles and burnt-out buildings multiplied. We would have appreciated off-road bikes or other practical vehicles, but no luck.

To the southeast squatted the forested mountains of North Cascades National Park. Blotching smoke plumed from their slopes, filling that quadrant of the sky, and angry flames followed the ridges. From our vantage, those fires appeared tiny, but they must have been fifty meters high. Nearer the lower drainages, half the trees were pale gray and dead, grave markers for ecosystems killed by two hundred years of bad forest management, runaway beetle kill, and climate change.

More forest fires waiting to happen.

They railway split from the road, and by the time I recognized the highway blockade, we were several hundred meters from it. Someone had stacked three levels of cars, three layers deep, on Highway 1 into Abbotsford. Whichever way Robert and his crew went, it wasn't through there, though they could have cut cross-country from Old Yale Road.

An overland route might have cost them serious time but, let's be clear, I hope we never see them again. Cuth's last words to us sounded something like COME NEAR ME AND I'LL KILL YOU.

Before the Third Pulse, we would have driven Interstate 5 through Bellingham, but most of 5 lies underwater with damn near every town along the coastal Pacific Northwest. Until Blight, new routes followed Highway 9, but it didn't take long before more blockades appeared along the smaller roads.

"Someone doesn't want people driving to the coast," Cailín said.

I pointed out that we were out of food and we might need to barter.

"Don't worry about the food," she said.

We paralleled the Valley Highway, farther from the coast, which brought us through treed foothills into a basin. On either side of an agricultural valley, rolling hills sprouted with luscious green copses and brittle, dry stands. This was a land clinging to life, failing.

At the valley's southern edge, black swathes of burnt woodland crossed west to east, climbing into the Cascades. A recent fire, already passed. Soot drew a line across the rails and highway, horizontal and absolute, like a Rothko painting. The sticks of burnt farmhouses jutted from the denuded ground.

To avoid burning to death, the safest ground in wildfire country is the ground already charred. At least we had that going for us.

We followed the blackened railroad line. Beside it, black tree trunks quilled the black earth, reeking of white ash. Smoke curled from hotspots which awaited winter or an unlikely rain to quench them. For stretches, the fire had grown so hot that it gutted the railroad ties and warped the steel. As the route ascended, the line once more paralleled the road, and here Cailín and I stopped.

Truck one, truck two, truck three.

As black as everything else, melted to their rims, nothing but husks. The fuel drums had exploded.

We approached slowly, crossing glassy, smooth, cool asphalt. Cailín neared the cavalcade from the left. I covered the right. Upholstery scorched from the seats, plastic melted from the dashboards and puddled on the floor, glass shattered. In three seats slouched the cracked, skeletal remains of former travelling companions. One retained only a single recognizable object—a warped cross on a metallic chain, shockingly clean and shiny.

Faith.

So much for faith.

In the seat beside her, I assumed, had been Robert. At least they died together. In the truck behind them, Frank's remains had fused with the steering wheel.

If we'd stayed with these people, would we have died too? My guess is Cuth or Frank would've killed us long before the fire did.

We didn't take long to ponder this before putting our feet back in motion.

XVII. INFECTION

DAY 186—

CAILÍN WASN'T KIDDING ABOUT food, which is good, because we have no guns, and I can't exactly throw a spear. Not well. We're weaponless, and not for lack of trying, since we searched three gun shops in Sedro-Woolley.

Sometime since the start of Blight, someone rounded up all the rifles and pistols in every town along Highway 9. No one needs that many guns, but it was a smart move—the guns you have are the guns others can't use against you.

More power to 'em.

On the topic of food, this is what Cailín does—

Rabbits are easiest. She calls them to her the same way she calls the ravens or the dog, and she's sweet to them, like a brunette Sleeping Beauty but without that stupid dances-with-the-animals scene. I've watched Cailín pat them on the top of the head before she breaks their necks.

Not any grimmer than shooting. Cleaner, too. It puts food in our stomachs, and it keeps us moving, saves hunting time, makes us nimble. I don't bother asking how she does it.

I already know.

Whatever it is that's in her, it's in me too, probably since our first kiss. After Blight, without question I accept the idea of new, strange, communicable diseases, this one included. The queer violet of her lips and tongue has appeared at the edges of mine, at the flesh on the floor of my mouth, and in more private places, spreading by the day. If it is something fatal, well, I guess we'll die. Six months on, though, and she's still breathing.

Each night, my dreams resonate more strongly. By day, the ground speaks more clearly beneath my feet. The sounds of animals do not translate into language—that isn't it, nothing Disney about it—but into a music whose chords and keys I interpret, which communicate patterns. On our first night together, I know why Cailín did not fear the fire, how the land whispered to her of its intentions.

What we feel isn't omniscience—Nature decides what She will decide—

It is insight.

A trimming of all possible futures.

This afternoon I called my first rabbit and broke its neck. How many deer have I shot? Shooting is less intimate, and the immediacy of those slight, breaking vertebrae and the last quiver of life shook me. I'm still trembling.

Why does the rabbit give up its life?

Why have I?

The sex tonight was fantastic. Every night, it gets better. Afterward, I lay with my head against her shoulder, my hand on her belly, and her body spoke to me the way the earth had been speaking to me.

ME:	You're pregnant.
CAILÍN:	I'm surprised you didn't already notice. There's a noticeable bump.
ME:	Whose is it?
CAILÍN:	Does that question make sense anymore?

She was right. Like hell am I dragging the patriarchy with me into the future, even if it isn't much of a future, even if everyone's dead in a few years anyway.

She's sleeping now. I'm sitting on a boulder overlooking the deadwood valleys of Colton. The moon is new, the night is black, and every tree on this mountainside is dead. To the southwest, there're streetlights in Salem. Tomorrow, we might try Salem, see if we can barter for a few helpful items.

Since civilization ended, the stars are much brighter. With relative ease, I spot several satellites and one of the orbital Stations, new moons going round and round and round the globe. Far away, loud but invisible to me, a StratoJumper pierces the upper atmosphere.

XVIII. PREACHER

DAY 187—

DO YOU KNOW ABOUT the Salem Witch Trials?

Apropos of this shitty day—

Moribund. Do you know the word?

It means something like "on the verge of death." It can also mean "stagnant" or "stuck."

During the Third Pulse, much of Salem, Oregon flooded, but people still live on its high ground. Before the Pulses, the city's population was maybe half a million. We never got close enough to count heads, but before descending to the flats, we studied Salem through my binoculars. Maybe three thousand people dwell there now, packed west of the Willamette River, which is no longer a river but a brackish inlet of the Pacific. The water and a partial barrier, similar to Prince George's, protect Salem from any overland attack. Built on pylons, a wooden bridge crosses the river, and active farmland radiates from both banks. The Pulses washed out much of Interstate 5 and the 99, but a newer dirt highway cuts north-south.

Every few meters, crucifixes stake the highway. They extend kilometers in either direction, more than a thousand crosses, each with its own Christ-like figure—like the Via Appia after Crassus defeated Spartacus, when moribund men lined the road from Rome to Capua.

If the dead weren't enough to intimidate—

While we watched, an explosion blossomed on the other side of the river. A magnificent blue flash hyper-lit the landscape, making even daylight dull, like an overexposed photograph. A repulsive brown plume peaked above the blast site, and a shockwave rippled across open ground. Five seconds later, a series of thunderous booms crashed past us.

"I suppose we can avoid Salem," Cailín said.

Rather than bearing due south, the rail bent southwest, too near the city, and so we bushwhacked. This veered us closer to the hills and their patchy stands of green, brown, and dead gray, then finally into cornfields. Taller than us, the corn blocked our view in every direction, but my compass kept us southward.

The afternoon brought with it a humid, pasty air. The corn stilled the breezes. Adding a wall of sound, cicadas croaked ceaselessly. No sight lines, the bugs masking any footfalls, a perfect setup for ambush.

Long before they reached us, though, we knew the Preacher's men were closing from the west. We knew this because the soil told us, because the corn muttered of them, and finally because the dog barked a warning. Let's be real— burgeoning supernatural abilities do not suck. We also knew that running for the hills would be the death of us, that like coyotes after frightened cats, they'd hunt us down.

We stayed, raising our arms in surrender.

Farmers by the look of them, a dozen emerged from the corn. Armed with rifles, shotguns, pistols.

The Preacher wore black, cleaned and pressed but sweat-soaked. His collar shone, pristine and white. His horn-rimmed glasses reflected the afternoon sunlight.

"Greetings," he said.

PREACHER: You two fine ladies got something
              against roads?

ME: I've had some terrible experiences on roads. We try to avoid them.

PREACHER: Nothing to fear near Salem. We have no murderers here. No rapists neither.

ME: That who we see hanging up on all those crosses? Murderers and rapists?

PREACHER: Some of 'em. Mostly, though, those are Ditchers.

CAILÍN: What exactly are Ditchers?

PREACHER: Ah! An Irish beauty! Lovely lilt you have there, my dear.

He waited for her response. None came, and his men shared uncomfortable glances. The Preacher smiled.

PREACHER: A Ditcher is someone intent on abandoning Earth, on tossing aside their personal responsibility for everything which has happened to the world, to their brothers and sisters. God created the Earth for mankind, and mankind has shit on God's creation since the invention of the steam engine. The Good Book makes it clear—you leave this world by going to Heaven or by going to Hell—ain't no other ways.

ME: And all those people you've nailed up, they were Ditchers?

PREACHER: Most of 'em. We don't put 'em on the cross without great deliberation, please understand. We have the rule of law. The Salem Ditch Trials, if you will.

ME: I see.

PREACHER: Most of 'em heading to San Francisco Island, have dreams of taking that so-called space elevator, the Corkscrew, to ride the abomination into the skies.

ME: And you stop them?

PREACHER: We'll stop 'em all soon. Have brave men down there already—the Moribund—heroes and revolutionaries. Men to bring down the false gods, to melt down the golden calf.

ME: Something to do with that explosion we saw?

PREACHER: As it happens, yes. A blessing from God.

ME: Was that a test?

PREACHER: A successful one.

ME: Hellelujah.

PREACHER: That's "hallelujah."

ME: Right.

PREACHER: A few others coming through have been Richies, stuck going overland, heading to Nevada. Less we can do about them, armed as they, but we catch 'em as we can.

CAILÍN: What's in Nevada?

PREACHER: Rumour is they're launching Strato-Jumpers from flats outside Reno.

ME: Well I'll be.

PREACHER: So what about you? Tell me. Where you ladies headin'?

Ever since Winnipeg, I have been studying maps of North America. I could remember markers for the plentiful military bases which dot Oregon, east of the highway—no doubt the source of the Preacher's blessing from God.

But at that moment, with the Preacher staring at me, with his men tapping their triggers, my mind blanked of everything else. For seconds, I couldn't remember a single town near Salem, anywhere I could name as a destination other than San Francisco. The only sound was the cicadas.

Finally I blurted, "Down to Albany, then to Sweet Home. I've got a sister there I lost contact with." I became conscious of my accent, wondered if I sounded too Canadian.

More cicadas.

PREACHER: That's a shame.
ME: Why?
PREACHER: Last we heard, Sweet Home was lost. Nobody left.
ME: I see. Maybe you can understand that me and my friend have got to try?
PREACHER: You'd be safer in Salem.
ME: Tell you what. We'll check out Sweet Home. If we don't find my sister, we'll come back.
PREACHER: I'll do you one better.

Cicadas loud like a 1970s rock band. Cicadas at one hundred thirty decibels.

"I'll send Jack with you," said the Preacher, gesturing to a chunky man. "He's got a truck. He'll escort you down the highway to Sweet Home all the quicker, then bring you back, your sister too if she's still alive."

Jack is almost two meters of buzzcut, square-jawed, raw muscle. Jack carries a giant shotgun. Jack would be an asset if he'd join our side—which he will never do.

Hearing the Preacher, Cailín pursed her lips, prepared a refusal.

I stepped forward. "Sounds wonderful, padre. It's about time we got a break."

The Preacher and his men escorted us southwest to the highway. Men and women hang on every cross out there, some barely bones, some rotting, some freshly dead. The smell made me gag.

Jack brought us to his oversized baby-blue pickup truck, and Cailín and I slid into the seat beside him. The dog rode in the bed. The ravens have dispersed, but Nevermore is never far away. I don't know how that bird keeps up with a vehicle, but as often as not, when I look out the window, there he is. Circling the sky. Sitting on a telephone pole. Plucking the eyes from the skulls of the crucified.

Jack noticed the bird too, and I'm afraid he might stop to take a potshot.

JACK:	What're you writing in that book of yours?
ME:	Nothing.
JACK:	Oh, don't give me that.
ME:	It's my diary.
JACK:	Bet there's some fun readin' in there.

Jerk.

For the first time since coming together, Cailín and I are careful to act like anything but a couple. Are the good people of Salem, Oregon the kind to stone a couple of queer girls to death?

I find it more than likely.

XIX. CORKSCREW

Day 189—

Jack carried his shotgun, a Glock, and a Bowie knife.

He drove an old Ford with a bench seat. I sat in the middle with the stick shift between my knees, and this often put Jack's hand uncomfortably near my crotch. Cailín rode in the passenger seat.

By the kilometer, the horror of Salem's power over the northwestern coast grew clearer. Cailín and I badly underestimated the breadth of their slaughter—the parade of the Jesusified extended the length of highway between Salem and Albany.

Signs between the crosses read:

THE LORD GIVETH, AND THE LORD
   TAKETH AWAY
WE DIE ON EARTH
   WHEN THE WORLD ENDS
THE WORLD ENDS WHEN WE END
   REJOICE FOR THE END
THE GOOD LORD COMES AT THE END
   ONE WORLD ENDS, ANOTHER BEGINS
MEET THE END WITH PRAYER
   WE'RE ALREADY DEAD, WE JUST DON'T
   KNOW IT YET
DITCHERS DESERVE TO DIE

In passing, we recognized Garret. Nailed up. Vulture meat. Cailín and I had the sense not to stare, letting the body pass.

"I know it's overwhelming," said Jack.

"Shocking, how so many would want to abandon their world," said Jack. "Give up on the rest of us. "

"Just remember," said Jack. "Their deaths are righteous."

Work crews and armed patrols saluted Jack's truck, which flew the Salem flag—a field of black, the green-blue orb of the Earth, and a golden cross jutting from the North Pole. Old FEMA trailers and mobile homes, spaced at half-mile intervals, gave these men shelter. At key locations, abandoned cars had been piled as defensive barriers.

No women in the crews. All at home, I suppose, barefoot and pregnant.

Pregnant made me think of Cailín, and I wanted to hold her hand. Jack might have perceived such a gesture as friendly. Might have taken it as romantic. Discretion is the better part of valor.

"Interesting color of lipstick you ladies wear," Jack said.

The highway curved east of Albany, intersecting with 20. We couldn't fly down the roads like we would have before Blight, but the entire drive to Sweet Home didn't amount to three hours. Along the way, I imagined grabbing the steering wheel and spinning us off the road, but a move like that was as likely to kill us and leave Jack alive. If we rolled, the dog would assuredly die.

But I knew Jack's job, and it wasn't to keep us safe. By the look in her eyes, Cailín understood it too.

As soon as we entered the ghost-town of Sweet Home, he asked, "Which way?"

"Right," I said.

"Left," I said.

"Right, left, right." I had no idea, prayed the turns brought us into a quiet neighborhood of abandoned houses where I might plausibly claim a house.

"That one," I said.

A picket-fence ranch house on 13th, painted green, with a long, simple gable. Two other houses on this block had burned down. Another's roof had collapsed.

Jack parked the truck.

"Let me go in by myself," I told him, packing my voice with trepidation, letting it tremble. This was about making him believe I knew this place, that my family might be inside.

He nodded, but insisted Cailín stay with him.

Through the white-painted gate, across a dandelion-riddled lawn, and to the door. I knocked, tried the knob, opened the door.

I recoiled from the stench. On a couch reclined two humanoid forms, bodies sprouting with tawny fungus, every centimeter of flesh hosting mushrooms which curved and stretched toward the ceiling. A wet, papery miasma rolled past me and I slammed the door shut.

I reached deep inside myself, tapped my own despair. My family's deaths. My old girlfriend's death. Raymond's death. The dead, nameless old man in Edmonton. I pulled the stops, let myself gibber, moan, finally scream. Tears erupted like pent-up lava flows. I ran onto the lawn, shaking my arms, hugging myself, jumping and wailing. It felt incredible, honestly, casting off the accumulated stress, fear, uncertainty, to do more than bite back tears and sniffle. I shrieked—

"They're dead! They're dead!"

Jack, the poor idiot, he ran to me. At first he didn't touch me, a shred of decency in him. I nurtured my charade, gave it full hysteria, gasping and hyperventilating. By now, Cailín stood beside me, and I'd confused her as much as him.

Finally he tried to wrap those manly arms around me. Got close. I slumped, gave him my weight until my cheek rested against his chest, still crying, moaning, keening.

His shotgun still in the truck. Glock at his right hip, knife at his left.

I pulled his pistol and pressed the muzzle under his chin. For an instant, I wondered whether it could end peacefully, maybe he'd lift arms, maybe we could have left him there and driven away with his vehicle—on foot it'd take him eight hours to reach the nearest of Salem's patrol stations, and by then we'd be long gone.

Instead he grabbed my wrist, his grip hateful, the pain like a branding iron. He twisted my bones like wet rags. Wouldn't have taken him much to yank my arm down.

I pulled the trigger.

I've been thinking about all the people I've killed.

After taking Jack's weapons and ammunition, we tore the Salem flag off the truck and drove south. Fifteen minutes down Marcola Road, I was giggling my head off, not because anything was funny but because my unstoppered emotions kept rolling from me. They flowed, and if I wasn't giggling I was going to collapse into a sobbing puddle.

We blew east of Eugene—no idea what's happening there—and within a couple of hours we were cruising Highway 5. We didn't stop until after midnight, south of what used to be Redding. Long ago this region succumbed to drought and perennial fires. Except arid grasses, there's not much left here to burn, which makes it an impossible place to live but a remarkably safe place to stop. We're off the road and I've returned to my old habit of no lights, no fires.

Cailín has wandered into the desert, and her sorcerous energy courses through the dry ground and the electric air. She's communing, ululating in a high, unearthly voice—trilling in a language which is no language, or maybe is the first of languages, and several times a deep rumble answers her from the wilderness.

No clouds.

No lightning.

No thunder anywhere.

As Cailín sings, I'm sitting on the tailgate of the truck, facing south.

Less than three hundred klicks between here and San Francisco. I swear the city's lights twinkle on the horizon, but I don't think that's physically possible. The lights of Avidità's space elevator, however, create a strange beacon which glances at an acute angle from the San Francisco Island and rises beyond imagining. Along its vector, safety bulbs blink on and off.

The Avidità Corkscrew, I heard once, reaches forty thousand kilometers into space. From the ground, we can't see more than the first twenty klicks. I figure at sunrise, though, we might glimpse more as the sun lights the elevator from the side.

Tonight, I fancy I can make out a few of the building-sized people-Carriers, corkscrewing up the elevator's Cogs. The Carriers don't come back down, but become part of the Goliath Stations which Avidità has constructed in orbit. The whole apparatus seems so implausible, so magical, and so surreal that for now I suspend all disbeliefs.

A baked, charred, dying land surrounds me. Cailín's serenading a God. Nevermore perches on a dead oak tree, and the dog lies beside me. The raven's ravenness and the dog's dogness exist in my senses as palpable things, amenable, malleable to the touch. I taste a new potential for life in every sweet breeze, draw its flavor along my darkly violet tongue. The world's energy whirls peaceably through me, a current which escapes time and of which I am a part.

I sit in a place between Gods.

In the north, Old Gods reawakening.

In the south, New Gods climbing their Towers from Babel.

Here at the middle-ground, happily, I am only mortal.

XX. VISIONS, PART III

A premonition—

White walls. White couches. White floor. White bathrooms. White bedrooms. White hallways. White furniture. White toothbrushes. White clothes. White lights.

Emerald accents. Patterned pillows. Charcoal cabinets. Mauve sheets. Silver utensils. Earthy orange plates. Enameled cookware.

Lightless outer space, as seen through clear diamondide windows.

No stars. We're too close to Earth's reflected glare, and this generates too many lumens, blotting any starshine.

I am riding in a cushioned, comfortable, enclosing chair on a Pod which is attached to a Carrier which is clipped to the Cogs which spiral around the spine which is the Corkscrew. Each Pod consists of four Rings. Once outside Earth's gravity, a Ring's rotation generates a centripetal equivalent of one gee for its passengers.

Each Pod rises at fifty kilometers per hour, and to reach our shuttle connections to the Orbiters will take thirty-three days. The energy required to ascend is less than a millionth of a twentieth-century rocket.

Cailín sits in the chair across from me, no longer dressed in leathers and furs but in a mint-green jumper, a vermillion scarf around her neck. Her lips, too, vermillion—makeup covering the violet of her mouth. Once long, Cailín's hair is now short and bobbed.

Next to her sits Sadzie, clothed similarly, her hair blacker than Cailín's. She wears a silver necklace, which I assume endemic to her tribe, but I don't really know. She smiles at me.

Beside me, Cuth settles in his seat, hands folded in his lap. He fidgets, worries his lip, and stares past me out the window, mesmerized by the Earth, which spins relative to our Pod. Some passengers can't watch out the windows or they throw up.

On one revolution, with Earth behind us, I glimpse our destination. The ship, formed like a double donut, hovers thousands of kilometers away but appears so god-sized it feels as if I could grab it like a frisbee.

An attendant brings tea and snacks. In a nearby play area, a group of children tussle. At a white table, two old farmers deal cards.

Seeing Cuth, how contented he is with me, with Cailín, with Sadzie, I know I'm dreaming.

Do inhibitions exist in dreams?

Cailín kisses Sadzie's cheek, and Sadzie gazes at me, her eyes darker than mine, like raw cocoa or rich mulch. This is her dream too, and she leans toward me.

Our kiss tastes sweet, and whatever reserve she may have harboured melts like a spring frost in five degrees of global warming. She eases into the kiss.

The Carrier shakes.

Lights flicker and a metallic boom beats our eardrums. The Pod rattles and spins. Angular momentum translates into terrifying force, throwing anyone not strapped down, smacking bodies into bulkheads. Someone's blood stipples my face.

The Corkscrew wobbles, bows, and breaks. Like a failing steel cable, but orders of magnitude more powerful, the line snaps, leaving the Carrier at the mercy of Earth's gravity. The jolt of free-fall ratchets my stomach into my throat.

"We're already dead," Cuth shouts, "we just don't know it yet!"

Another boom, and the Carrier tilts. Fire wraps its shell. The Carrier swims in fire. The omnipresent fire brightens with atmospheric friction, the fatal drag of re-entry.

SADZIE:	I'm scared.
ME:	Don't be. You're dreaming.
CAILÍN:	But this is one probable future. Don't forget.
CUTH:	The Good Lord comes at the end!

Shear forces rip the Carrier to pieces. Death is instantaneous.

XXI. PROCESSING

Day 191—

Any day might be my death day, but at the moment I'm eating a croissant and drinking great coffee. The half-and-half, they say, comes from artificial udders, grown in orbital facilities. People surround me, better fed and more rested than any I've seen in months—though everyone has the fractionally dark, slightly sunken look of PTSD. More than a hundred years ago, PTSD was "shell shock."

I am shell-shocked.

Shell-shocked on San Francisco Island.

Otherwise crystalline blue, to the west the ocean sports an eggplant-hued smear which floats north to south, several kilometers long and three or four klicks from shore. Jellyfish blooms—abundant in today's sea. Beautiful waters, but don't swim them.

Before Pulse Three, we could have driven from Redding to San Francisco in a few hours. For us, rounding the Inland Central Sea cost two days and, from the north, only one road led to Oakland. Along it, competing signs declared:

(On plywood, spray-painted by the Moribund)
MEET THE END WITH PRAYER
DITCHERS DESERVE TO DIE
SINNERS BURN IN HELL
GOD SAVES

(Or with designed lettering on powder-coated steel)
IN SAN FRANCISCO,
ESCAPE A DYING EARTH
AND SAVE THE HUMAN RACE.
AVIDITÀ CORPORATION WELCOMES ALL.

Twice, we siphoned petrol from derelict cars and old service pumps. Driving into San Francisco proper was no longer possible, since the last Pulse metamorphosed the city's heart into an island—or an archipelago defined by Mt. Davidson and the Twin Peaks, Los Pechos de la Chola.

Instead, Cailín and I arrived in Oakland, near the waterline.

If Prince George had a self-proclaimed Prince, then San Francisco has an actual King. King Avidità founded Avidità Corporation, then became the CEO of a multinational conglomerate. After Pulse Three, he ascended as the unquestioned monarch of one of the world's largest capitalist powerhouses. During the Pulses, he pooled resources into the California coast—a drone airforce, agricultural towers, desalination plants, solar arrays, wind farms, thorium reactors, and the Corkscrew, a wonder of technology reaching into space. The Corkscrew's azimuth angled due south, as high as anyone can see, vertical elevation at fifty-two degrees.

An escalator to heaven?

My mind boggled at it, so close and in full daylight, its structure rising from platforms on waters south of the islands. On the waters around it floated a thousand Carriers, waiting in queue for their turns to rise. Out to sea, gargantuan facilities constructed more Carriers. Surely, this was a surrealist's fakery? An LSD fantasy? If I blinked, would it disappear? If I clicked my heels twice, would I return to Winnipeg?

Every three hours, a Carrier began its assent, cradling a thousand people in its Pods. Each Carrier the volume of an old-fashioned cruise ship, one after the other they latched onto the Corkscrew's Cog system and spiraled upward into a month-long ride to the orbital Stations.

Beside me, Cailín drank tea with milk, no sugar. She kept glancing over her shoulder, a tick fueled by justified paranoia. Plenty to fuel it.

Where was Cuth? In town, somewhere, itching to make good on his promise.

And where were the Moribund?

In the alleyways or on the corners of half-drowned buildings, the Preacher's devotees left their spray-painted graffiti:

DITCHERS DESERVE TO DIE
 AVIDITÀ WILL BURN IN HELL
  REJOICE! FOR THE END IS COME
   THE GOOD LORD COMES AT THE END

Yesterday, in Oakland, we surrendered our vehicle to King Avidità's security teams. Farther down the coast, a processing plant crushes cars into heavy blocks. Other machines stack these blocks and weld them, transforming them into the most impressive defensive wall I've seen yet.

Avidità's security confiscated our weapons too.

Last, they took the dog.

"Quarantine," they said.

"You'll get him back in a month," they said.

A customs and naturalization officer recorded our names and birthplaces. Officers scanned our retinas, took our fingerprints, noted our vitals, and drew blood.

ME:	What's the blood for?
OFFICER:	DNA, organ function, disease panels.
ME:	Diseases like what?
OFFICER:	Cancer, HIV, anemia, heart disease, blood parasites, a host of others.
ME:	Blight?
OFFICER:	Everyone has Blight, even if it doesn't kill them. Cure's coming, though.

Before releasing us, they slipped GPS trackers under the skin at the back of our necks. After processing, we rode a shiny, new monorail across the Bay into San Francisco. High tech, maglev, complete with security drones and CopBots to ensure we behaved.

In the train car, standing at the other end, Cuth and Sadzie were staring at us.

In the wilderness, we'd have drawn weapons and proceeded to kill each other, but here the protocols of civilization kicked in. Sadzie gawked at me—not the mere recognition of a past travelling companion, but the remembrance of intimacy, a shared phantasmagoria, even if in dreams. She looked away.

Cuth stepped forward, leaned in, and spoke against my ear.

"Your girlfriend's a goddamned witch who has to die," he said, "and looks like you are now too."

I told him to go fuck himself and die.

"I promise I'm going to kill you both," he said. "You'll never make it off this island."

The train arrived at a sparkling terminal, still under construction, robotic builders tirelessly completing their tasks. From the train cars, hundreds of people dispersed through an atrium, and Avidità's representatives greeted us. They arranged temporary housing, food, water, medicine, and counseling. Cailín and I held hands, gaining our bearings.

In the crowds, we lost track of Cuth and Sadzie.

A young man, our representative wore a finely printed navy suit, fashioned by CAD/CAM, which shouted of wealth. Unbelievable, to walk through six months of blood-washed wilderness, and now to stand in the mouth of opulence.

"I'll be your liaison," he told us, "until we get you boarded onto a Carrier. First thing, I'll take you to your hostel."

We thanked him, neither of us quite believing him. I've gone through enough shit, heard enough lies, and I'm guessing I'll have trust issues for the rest of my life. Cailín, up there with the Horned Lords, she suffered far worse than I.

"May I ask," said our host, glancing at our joined hands, "are you married?"

San Francisco had long been a bastion of same-sex rights. Seemed that remained so. I wondered what special resources a married couple might claim—there were always some.

ME:	Yes, yes, we are.
CAILÍN:	Wifeys.

No private vehicles on San Francisco Island. By sunset we rode in an autonomous car which tracked with hundreds of others, carrying us along Market Street, around Twin Peaks, to our accommodations.

Humble as it was, to us the hostel was a palace of Cleopatras. In Prince George, I'd worried how Raymond and I had fought, how our shouting might've bothered the neighbors. I'm sure Cailín and I bothered the neighbors too—

But for much different reasons.

XXII. BOMBING

ONE PART SHINING CITY of the Space Age, one part gilded twentieth-century city, one part New Venice, San Francisco of the early twenty-second century dazzles me and rocks me to my core. Kilometer-high towers of tensile carbon and titanium cast blanketing shadows across the central island's streets. Beneath them, historic edifices date from months after the 1906 earthquake, each structure immaculate. Around the intertidal zones, reinforced brick or concrete buildings continue to exist with two or three storeys under-water, canals navigable by vaporetti.

The San Francisco Islands bustle. Per square kilometer, more humans live here than in Manhattan at the height of that city's power. This late in the season, under the towers' shade, people can walk the city, go about their busi-ness, socialize. Otherwise, this far south, parallel with the Gobbling Desert, midday temperatures can reach forty-four Celsius, forty-eight on the eastern edges of the Central Sea. The farther south and inland, the deadlier the land becomes, and it worsens every year.

At what used to be Highway 280, a shallow inlet pene-trates San Francisco Island. A quay fronts this inlet from the old thoroughfare to the eastern grid of Excelsior, and at its southwest point is the Outer Mission Wharf.

This morning, several blocks northeast of the Outer Mission, Cailín and I were trading for supplies and clothing. San Francisco uses currency—printed and digital—and in two days we've managed to acquire more gear than either of us have owned since the coming of Blight, one hundred ninety-three days ago. Most San Franciscans are in queue to ride the Corkscrew, and people are giving away supplies which a week ago I would've killed for.

I ducked before I even realized why, reaching for Cailín, clinging to her.

The Wharf exploded, leveling four buildings and killing hundreds.

Along Monterey Boulevard, windows rattled and a thousand merchants and customers covered their ears. Wild survival instincts returned in a rush. Dust rolled through the district. Emergency responders, drones, and robots hurried past.

A terrorist attack, said the reports.

The Moribund, they said.

Old tunnels beneath the streets, forgotten chambers, drainages which empty below the new waterline—the bots and artificial intelligences can't secure every route into the city. In their attacks, the Moribund haven't damaged the Corkscrew—

—"The terrorists cannot hurt the infrastructure," say the authorities.

"They cannot harm the Corkscrew," they say.—

—but the Wharf's destruction has pinched supply lines. This'll slow the preparation of Carriers, keep more people stranded Earth-side for longer. Within hours, the city rerouted boat traffic, distributing it amongst several dozen smaller ports, and Avidità announced new, tougher checks on incoming sea vessels.

The wharf burned most of today and, to douse the flames, the response teams positioned house-sized saltwater pumps along the inlet. Whatever weapon the Moribund had used, it wasn't fertilizer-based or some other home-brew explosive.

Cailín and I had seen it before. The Preacher's blessing from God, tested outside Salem, now delivered right here to San Francisco.

XXIII. THE BLOOD REMAINS

Day 205—

Using the hostel's bathroom sink, I scrubbed blood from beneath my fingernails. Some, more stubborn, still clings there. Maybe it always will?

I'm thinking about all the dead in the world. How much blood on my hands?

In high school, I played Lady MacBeth. Messed-up material for teenagers, but our teacher predicted the end of the world, that she wanted us prepared for dark days.

> *Out, damned spot! Out, I say!—One, two. Why,*
> *then, 'tis time to do 't. Hell is murky!—Fie, my*
> *lord, fie! A soldier, and afeard? What need we*
> *fear who knows it, when none can call our power to*
> *account?—Yet who would have thought the old man*
> *to have had so much blood in him.*

Last night, on a crowded street, Cailín and I found an akachōchin noodle bar, a place with farm-raised or vat-grown fish, I'm not sure which. The bar's red lantern welcomed us in. At the counter, some withered guy said fish doesn't taste as wholesome as it used to, but neither Cailín nor I are old enough to have ever eaten much ocean-caught fish anyway. The vegetables were amazing—sprouted in ag towers within San Jose, walled off from the sea.

CAILÍN: I'm so hungry.
ME: You're eating for two.

Best she can figure she's in week fifteen, showing for anyone with eyes to see. She wolfed down one bowl, slurping her noodles, then ordered a second with extra carrots. While she ate, I chatted with other patrons. Few were native San Franciscans. People have come from as far away as Monterrey, Mexico or Omaha, Nebraska, everyone bearing their own traumas.

The man behind the bar turned up his stereo. It was blaring old electronica. Most of it I didn't recognize, but there was a bunch of twentieth-century soundscape lusciousness, heavy on the synthesizers. Tangerine Dream, Vangelis, some obscure Irisarri.

Like a recurring dream, "When the World Ends" played again.

When I first left Winnipeg, I weighed about eight kilos too many. By the time I arrived at San Francisco, the med-techs called me "malnourished" and told me to up the calories—as if I'd spent the last six months on a fad diet.

We paid for what we ate, but this wasn't difficult— many San Franciscans trade goods or labor for more money, but Avidità supplies Islanders with a universal basic income, and the hostel charges no rent. The Corporation treats us as refugees and, from our lowly position, Avidità is a benevolent Caesar. That the city works so efficiently, and cleanly, testifies to his power.

After dinner, Cailín and I wandered. Flâneur, the French say. San Francisco offered us an endless palimpsest, beautiful and varied. A few surviving hints of pre-1906 architecture shown through, along with swathes of Victoriana overarched by twenty-first century excesses and Avidità's twenty-second-century wonders. In this Corporate City, the tallest carbon buildings reach to more than a kilometer, multiples over the partially drowned Transamerica Pyramid, whose upper storeys still function, lights glowing through the windows.

Though still populous, Francisco is emptying—fewer live here than a year ago, steadily riding the escalator to heaven—the Stations are that voluminous. Avidità estimates their capacity at twelve million.

The old International Space Station had, what, a capacity of ten, as in one-zero, as in less than a dozen?

We strolled Golden Gate Park, which remains a park, lush green and vibrantly alive, maintained with desalinated water. The risen ocean drowned the park's western half, where new docks host yachts whose lights reflect romantically from water. The yachts remind me of Raymond, of his plan to take a boat and follow the coast up to Anchorage.

Trees shelter the rest of the park, and their leaves murmured in a cool nighttime breeze. While hundreds of promenaders enjoyed the grasses and trees, space enough exists in the park to let people whisper with each other, talk without shouting, hold hands, frolic. After months of travelling through necropolises, though, even Golden Gate feels busy.

Yet safer. I almost relaxed.

Tracing their grid, Avidità's CopBots hovered unobtrusively. A year ago, had deployments like this monitored Winnipeg, I'd have been screaming about Big Brother. Last night, I appreciated someone else doing the watching.

Stupid.

Cuth slipped his knife into Cailín's back, below her ribs. Pierced a kidney.

She screamed and her pain was mine. Right to my own teeth, the empathetic jolt froze me, pinned me to the soles of my shoes.

On the second blow, Cuth's blade found my sternum. It clunked into the bone, and a fractional moment passed while neither of us understood why I wasn't dead. Shocking pain spread from my chest, up my neck, down my belly.

I kicked him in the balls, drove the air from his lungs, and he stumbled back. He reached for me, I shoved him away, and the fucking knife wobbled, the handle dropping a few centimeters. A few hundred grams, that knife, and the bone wouldn't let it go.

Cailín was still screaming—not panic but agony.

Diving, Cuth snatched me around the middle. His weight twice mine, he could've hoisted me WrestleMania-style. Yet he slipped, dropped to one knee, and he was strong but my thighs have walked thirty-five hundred kilometers.

He reached for the knife handle—

—I was faster.

The CopBots flanked us, blaring: "Citizens, cease fighting. On your knees with your hands in the air."

Bell-like, the knife blade rang when I jerked it from my breastbone. Cuth slapped me down, my back hit the lawn, and his arms encircled my waist. His clunky head butted my abdomen as he squeezed—two of my ribs broke—

"Citizens—"

I jammed the blade into the meat beside Cuth's neck, shoving the point behind the clavicle. I pushed and blood spurted.

The CopBots fired.

My body went rigid and my jaw locked. Electricity short-circuited me from my eyeballs to my toes. Cailín was whimpering. Cuth was silent.

I woke this morning in a hospital.

XXIV. BROKEN PROMISES

Day 205—

In the wilderness, Cailín would have died.

Instead, a huge, four-rotor, AI-driven medevac whisked her from the green and lifted her to a hospital. High in one of the carbon towers, med-techs stopped the bleeding, stabilized her, and printed her a new kidney.

I compare this to my last half year. To the premium I placed on bandaids, gauze, and antibiotics. I forget who, but some futurist of the last century said that technology improves, costs less, and becomes more widely distributed over time, that technologies tend toward ubiquitousness.

In capitalism, only when ubiquitousness is profitable.

Here on San Francisco Island, Avidità has hoarded technology for decades. Half the gadgets here I've heard about but never imagined I'd see. Wonders fully formed, magical apparatuses. Avidità might as well be Zeus.

A two-centimeter gash tore the skin between my breasts, and Cuth's knife chipped my sternum. Two floors down from where Cailín received her new kidney, a doctor and his AI Assist fixed my knife wound tout de suite, along with my broken ribs.

All I feel is sore and, in a whopping three days, they'll release Cailín too.

Cuth, they said, will need weeks. I missed his heart, but the knife clipped an artery, punctured a lung, and severed a mess of tissue. Before I left the hospital, an officer visited me. He tipped his bowler hat at me.

OFFICER: I'm Detective Azzo Melk.

ME: How much trouble am I in?

OFFICER: None. Everyone who comes here has had some fucked-up experiences. Up north, out in the Wastes, on the seas. All the same, all desperate, all violent. Hardly anyone makes it to Oakland who hasn't witnessed a lot of death.

ME: What're you saying?

OFFICER: We see a mental-health issue where you see a criminal act. Besides, most of your scuffle with Mr. Richards—

ME: Who?

OFFICER: Cuthbert. The drones videoed your fight. You acted in self-defense, especially considering his attack on your wife.

Wife. That makes me smile.

OFFICER: We're releasing you.

ME: Can I go up to Cailín's room?

OFFICER: Of course, but I recommend you go back to your hostel first, get your belongings.

ME: Why?

OFFICER: Refugees arriving daily. We'll free up your room, find you something more comfortable for the rest of your stay.

ME: Rest of our stay?

OFFICER: You're in queue to ride the Corkscrew. Mr. Avidità wants everyone topside by December twenty-one twenty-seven. That's a helluva timetable.

ME:	How long before our number comes up?
OFFICER:	Three months max.
ME:	So soon?
OFFICER:	In consideration for your wife's pregnancy. Mr. Avidità's orders—expecting women and parents of young children get priority.
ME:	All right. You know, Cuth—the guy you call Mr. Richards—he promised he'd kill Cailín, me too. Promised.
OFFICER:	Sometimes promises are broken. Sometimes that's all right.

While walking back to the hospital, I found my eyes drawn to the Corkscrew, asking myself why we'd come here. Ever since Raymond died, I've had it my head—

California or bust.

Ride the Corkscrew.

Reach the stars. Or Low Earth Orbit.

—but now the doubts are settling in, making themselves at home. Cailín has never offered her opinion on whether riding the Corkscrew is good or bad. "I dreamed my path," she said, "and my path is with you."

In the hospital, she's down the hall. They're testing her new kidney, and I have nothing to do but wait. In the recovery room, I make myself at home too, sit with the fay clicks and whirs and beeps of high-tech medical equipment. In the corner, a recliner overlooks the city and the Pacific.

We're ninety-four storeys up, and from here the line blurs between ocean and sky. Already dreamlike, this reality, and so I settle back in the chair and close my eyes.

XXV. VISIONS, PART IV

A PROPHECY—

ISLANDS NOT SO FAR south of the Arctic circle, but far enough that thick evergreen forests blanket a rocky land—clouds pillow the sky, dappling and desaturating the sunlight. Our long, clinker-built ship nears the shore, rowed by strong men and women. Cold waves slap the hull, and oars grind and squeak at each stroke.

From the mast flutters our banner, its coal-hued field stark behind a round emblem. Within the emblem, a jagged, dancetty line separates weaves of rich violet and bright gold.

Below the banner, the ship's black, rolled, fastened sails cast a cruciform shadow. Cailín stands at the helm in a dress of fluttering black, her toddler at her feet, a child with a bramble of hair as thick as her mother's. I sit at the rudder, steering us into a tranquil inlet bracketed by temperate rainforests. A short skirt of blanched wool wraps my hips, and my hand-sewn blouse flutters, a garment of translucent white with buttons of antler.

Tree limbs overarch us, darkening the light. The leaves and needles of oaks, tamaracks, cedars, birches, firs, lodge-poles, and maples brush the flanks of our ship. Its prow touches a sand bank, and the sailors jump the sides and pull us onto shore.

On any other day, our shield-bearers would accompany us overland, spears at the ready. Pirating southward, we might've taken a powered boat and firearms, but this is a sacred land and a sacred day. Nothing of the modern world can touch it—we leave modernity behind us.

Unescorted, Cailín and I proceed into the interior. Cailín's daughter remains with the shield-bearers.

"Bettina!" she cries for me. The child knows more words every day, too many for her age, and one of her first was my name.

A shield-bearer attempts to soothe her. Today, I do not look back.

Cailín walks ahead. The forest unfolds before us, each vista hidden until we step past a clatter of mossy boulders or ivy-clothed trees. Squirrels chatter at us. Ravens circle curiously, and Nevermore is never far away. A whiff of cedar smoke draws us forward, a campfire at the center of a circle of standing stones.

The stones are crisply worked, white granite, like gods' teeth.

An oak looms beyond the circle. Many-colored ribbons dangle from its branches, some waving in the breeze, others weighted with sticks. The sticks form unsettling patterns I do not comprehend.

From the thickest branches hang nine armless corpses, nooses tight around their necks.

Nodens welcomes us.

He is a man and no man, a black and specific presence which sits beside the fire but sits throughout the land but sits inside us. He is handsome and horrifying, naked but armored. He is a wolf but a bear but a moose but an owl but a caribou but a cougar but most of all a raven.

I realize—he's been travelling with us all along.

As we enter the circle he stands, taller than any man. He greets Cailín with a kiss, then enfolds me in his arms.

"Cherished," he says.

"Blessed," he says.

"Commander," he says.

"Of what?" I ask.

"Of every army to come."

"To fight against?"

"The New Gods themselves."

"How?"

"Teach her," says the God to the corpses, and the corpses open their mouths to speak.

Every word they utter shatters me, reframes the world, gives reality a new meaning. I can think only of modern metaphors: they rewrite me; they encode me; they re-parse me. Same hardware, altered program.

Within the circle, beside the fire, Nodens undresses me—away with the white. Undresses Cailín—away with the black. Undresses himself, which means he strips away all his disguises. He is present with us, as he was beside the dreamland fire in the wilderness west of McBride, though he wore Raymond's face then.

He claims us, and the joy is euphoric.

XXVI. WE DIE ON EARTH

Day 245—

WHAT WAS THE MORAL of "Jack and the Beanstalk"? I'm not sure, but I remember the beanstalk had to come down.

During these last six weeks, two more bombings rocked San Francisco. The first annihilated a processing facility on the Potrero Islet, killing dozens. The second shattered a crowded market, killing hundreds. The city's mood has darkened—the paranoia of the wilderness has invaded, and the veneer of civilization has cracked. Avidità pours resources into identifying agents of the Moribund, into bottling up any remaining smugglers' pipelines.

Terrorist attempts on the train station and Corkscrew platform failed. Officers captured five of the Preacher's faithful, escorted them to Mr. Avidità. No one has seen them since.

We did see Cuth.

On the street, he looked terrified to see us. He jammed his hands into his pockets, kept his head down, and passed us by. A collar encircled his neck, a sleek device, something high-tech and locked in place.

Sadzie confronted us outside a Lamaze class on Irving Street.

"Get your bad medicine out of my head," she told us.

"I'm not one of you," she said. "I'll never be one of you."

"I don't want anything to do with you." She was blubbering, her words as much about convincing herself as telling us anything. "I'm heading up the Corkscrew tomorrow, and I hope I never see you again."

That was two days ago.

She would have been about twelve hundred klicks up when explosions finally hammered the Corkscrew's platform and ripped its tensile roots from their moors, when the mega-structure jolted upward, then undulated, a godly dragon of mindless carbon fiber and titanium. Forty thousand kilometers of high-tensile material unleashed its force in a wave.

Imagine being a dust mite. Imagine you witness the cracking of a bullwhip.

A monstrous, glass-shattering, ear-splitting shriek blasted the islands, the Corkscrew lifted into the atmosphere as if it might take flight, then skyscraper-sized lengths of it fell to Earth. One struck the hills east of Oakland, throwing debris a kilometer into the sky. Dust clouds rolled across the Bay and choked its New Venice.

By then, Cailín and I figured what was coming. We took an auto as far as we could, then on foot climbed Mt. Davis, hurrying up its side as quickly as Cailín could. So many people stayed in the streets, awestruck by what confronted them, heading to the waterline to gawk at the plumes or the kilometers-long Corkscrew, freed from its restraints and yielding to drag and the angular momentum of a planet.

More skyscrapers pounded into the waters.

Water rushed from the intertidal zones. For a heart-stopping few seconds, whole neighborhoods of drowned San Francisco revealed themselves. Seaweed beds. Nascent coral, unbleached. Sunken houses and sunken lives.

Then the tsunami struck. Thirty meters high, it devoured streets spared during the Pulses. The waves roared, a million lions in unison.

Still, my wife and I climbed. I tugged her with me. We weren't alone. Thousands made it to Mt. Davis or the Twin Peaks, scrambling for high ground. I glanced over my shoulder.

Dirty brown water scoured every historic building, every warehouse, every street-level storefront or market. They're saying the death toll is thousands.

For so many survivors, it's just another tragedy. One more punch to the gut. Cailín and I collapsed next to a half-buried, cracked, century-old concrete wall. The graffiti on it read:

WE DIE ON EARTH.

Down in the city, Avidità's carbon-tensile super-towers did nothing more than wobble, the tsunami merely dabbing their toes. The Moribund brought the Corkscrew down, but San Francisco will live on.

It took hours for the water to drain back to the sea. Bots and volunteers wasted no time in the search for the injured and the trapped, in the collection of the dead.

We returned to our apartment in the Avidità Corporate Tower, one hundred ten storeys up. The dog—returned to us and healthier than on arrival—peed on the carpet while we were gone. It's almost midnight, and thankfully Cailín is sleeping peacefully.

An hour ago, the door chime rang. A visitor, our liaison. He dressed as smartly as he had the first time we'd met.

ME:	Late, isn't it?
LIAISON:	I was quite glad your name didn't make it onto the list of the dead.
ME:	Us too.
LIAISON:	Do you need anything?
ME:	Only sleep.
LIAISON:	I'll let you be. But first I come bearing a message.

ME:	Yes?
LIAISON:	Mr. Avidità requests your company in the morning. Breakfast will be served.
ME:	Requests?
LIAISON:	Perhaps "requests" isn't the right word.

The liaison is long gone. I fixed myself a cup of chamomile, and in a few minutes I'll join Cailín. The dog will sleep at our feet. One hundred ten storeys down, rescue operations and cleanup crews are working in earnest, still counting the dead, remaking order for the living. From this height, the loudest machinery produces only a faint, unreal hum.

One more crisis. One more collective refusal to give up.

Survive long enough, through enough catastrophe, and neither survival nor death much surprise anymore. Day by day the shock and overwhelm fade. All these near-death-experiences leave me with is gratitude for this moment.

In the morning, we'll have breakfast with a New God.

XXVII. BREAKFAST WITH GOD

Day 246—

I'VE BEEN THINKING ABOUT eggs Benedict.

Mr. Avidità's penthouse struck me as restrained and tasteful, in the way the ultra-rich can exhibit a refined palate with the ability to spend tasteless sums on simple things. We ate in a spacious dining room with four-meter-high ceilings. Two walls of reactive pigments shifted by imperceptible degrees between images by Gustav Klimt and Georg Fritz.

Along the facing walls, a sequence of delicate, silver mullions clasped slender, vertical windows. The delicacy and slenderness were illusory—the panes were several layers of diamondide separated by vacuum, missile-proof and insulated. Nearly two kilometers up, the penthouse's height inured it from humdrum, horrific, everyday events. The coastlines stretched a hundred sixty klicks north and south, the California interior shown on the other side of the Central Sea, and the Pacific glittered to the horizon.

We wore new dresses of blue, lab-grown cotton. Cailín had braided her hair.

Mr. Avidità took his seat at the end of the long table. His neatly trimmed navy suit, his tie, his brown monk-strap shoes—these fit him as comfortably as pajamas, as if he'd slept in them but then awoken perfectly groomed, as if he never wore anything less. He looked no more than forty—impossible because my dead parents had talked about how Avidità became powerful when they were teenagers.

He was goddamned handsome. Two robots accompanied him—four-legged things like headless mastiffs, surfaced with mirrored chrome. They sat obediently behind him.

No shit—he called them Ares and Apollo.

I got my eggs Benedict. Cailín ordered bacon rashers, pork sausage, two fried eggs, white pudding, buttered brown-soda toast with fried tomatoes, baked beans, and potatoes. Our host had a salad with poached eggs.

A chef conjured everything we wanted. Dressed in actual livery, kitchen staff served us as if we were queens.

CAILÍN:	It's not every day I meet someone famous. Avidità was a household name in Dublin.
AVIDITÀ:	I used to be a household name everywhere—I doubt that's true anymore.
ME:	Certainly true in San Francisco.
AVIDITÀ:	San Francisco, my own little fiefdom.
CAILÍN:	The breakfast is excellent, Mr. Avidità. Can't remember the last time I tasted rashers but, putting that aside, why have you brought us here?
AVIDITÀ:	It's not every day I encounter something new.
ME:	Something new?
AVIDITÀ:	Biologically, neither of you are entirely human.
ME:	Of course we are.
AVIDITÀ:	You're not. You remember we collected blood samples?
CAILÍN:	What're you saying?

AVIDITÀ:	Please don't play coy, ladies. More than a few San Franciscans have commented on the unusual color of your lips, and I noted it the first time I encountered your images.
ME:	Spying on your citizenry?
AVIDITÀ:	Keeping tabs on anomalies. My Director of Research drew my attention to your blood results, and since then we have watched you extremely carefully.
ME:	Why?
AVIDITÀ:	He wanted to quarantine you, but the data didn't support his fears.
CAILÍN:	What fears?
AVIDITÀ:	That you were carrying a new pathogen, something on the order of Blight, that you'd infect the population. I thought he might wet himself over it, but you've been here two months, and my hypothesis has won out.
ME:	What was your hypothesis?
AVIDITÀ:	That what you're carrying is sexually transmitted, and that you're not the most promiscuous young women on these islands.
ME:	What are we carrying?
AVIDITÀ:	An adaptive parasite. Symbiont might be a better word. Jury's still out on that one.
CAILÍN:	What does it do?
AVIDITÀ:	I was hoping you could tell me.

We explained that, there in the artifice of his tower or walking the city's streets, our senses told us little. In San Francisco, the tether between Cailín and I remained strong—we walked in each other's dreams as often as we walked together on the city's avenues—but our connection to nature became fraught.

In the open wilderness, though, amongst the grasses and trees, the land suffused us. Like spiders in our web, we knew the footfalls of men before they reached us. Beasts announced their presence, and their migrations stretched across the horizon, filaments which conveyed faraway events to our inner eyes. The winds delivered news from every direction.

Neither of us went as far as to tell him how we glimpsed the future, that we had foreseen the fall of his precious Corkscrew. We didn't explain projecting dreams into other people's heads. We didn't mention Old Gods in the north.

AVIDITÀ: You're basically communing with nature?
ME: I suppose.
AVIDITÀ: How very Dungeons and Dragons. Too bad. In case you hadn't noticed, Earth is dying, and soon there won't be much nature with which you can commune.

Tree limbs overarch us, darkening the light. The leaves and needles of oaks, tamaracks, cedars, birches, firs, lodgepoles, and maples brush the flanks of our ship.

Earth isn't dying, I thought.

Earth just underwent chemotherapy.

Earth is feeling like shit, but it's purging its cancer.

"I'm sorry the terrorists blew up your Corkscrew," I said, wanting then to flee the penthouse, to run back into the wilds, to travel as far north as I could.

AVIDITÀ:	The real loss is human life. No exact count, to be honest, but three hundred thousand people died yesterday.
ME:	So many?
AVIDITÀ:	Thousands killed in the tsunami, but the Corkscrew was like Hiroshima and Nagasaki combined. Eight Carriers a day, a thousand people per Carrier, a thirty-three-day trip. The math is straightforward. Even with this elevator, realistically, it was going to take us another four years to evacuate the islands. At least the incoming refugees have slowed to a dribble.
ME:	Poor Sadzie.
AVIDITÀ:	Sadzie?
ME:	A friend of ours—on your Corkscrew.
AVIDITÀ:	I'm sorry.
ME:	Earth is dying, you say. Why do you care? Why so motivated to get that many people onto your proverbial lifeboats?
AVIDITÀ:	Since you mention lifeboats—when the *Titanic* struck its iceberg, the engineering crew stayed at their posts. If they hadn't kept the pumps working, the ship would have sunk all the quicker. They kept the electricity on, too. Without it, the emergency radio couldn't transmit.

	Had those engineers shirked their duties, everyone aboard the *Titanic* would have died—the engineers included.
CAILÍN:	I'm guessing the engineers died anyway?
AVIDITÀ:	In a sense, the engineers were dead the moment the liner collided with the ice.
CAILÍN:	Are you an engineer, Mr. Avidità?
AVIDITÀ:	From the start of my career, madame.
ME:	What will you do now that the Corkscrew has fallen?
AVIDITÀ:	I have five more, other locations. I'll increase their security, since Salem's Moribund obviously discovered a weakness. We'll learn from this incident, improve as we always do. We're weighing whether rebuilding this Corkscrew is worth the expense, or whether we can funnel San Franciscans to the other locations, pick up the slack some other way.
ME:	What about the Moribund? If they strike again, keep bombing the city, keep up the propaganda?

Avidità ate the last of his eggs, then mopped the yolk with dry toast.

"Salem, Oregon no longer exists," he said. "At four o'clock this morning, my drones wiped it from the map, along with every military facility within two hundred miles of it. We scorched the fields."

ME: There were women there. Children.
AVIDITÀ: I know, right? Terrible.
ME: And still?
AVIDITÀ: When a few thousand moronic reli-
               gious zealots murder a quarter million
               innocents, I have no problem putting
               them down. I should have razed Salem
               months ago.
ME: That's a lot of death. Eye for an eye?
AVIDITÀ: To survive this year, how many people
               have you killed?

Our silence told him all he needed to know.

"For two years," he said, "I've been perfecting a facial-recognition map of everyone living along the coast between here and the Seattle Islands." He gulped the rest of his coffee. "Using that map, I trained my drones and two thousand K-bots—" He gestured to Ares and Apollo, by way of example. "—and these are now hunting the coast for anyone associated with Preacher Johnson or the Moribund. One or two may escape, but the Preacher and his sheep are extinct."

The waitstaff whisked away the plates, then refilled our water glasses and coffee cups.

AVIDITÀ: The disease you carry is fascinating.
               It's engineered. How you came by it,
               Cailín, up there in the north with those
               Horned Lords—that's only part of the
               story, and I'd like to unravel the rest.
CAILÍN: Which means you want to study us?
AVIDITÀ: I'm not talking about rats in a cage
               here. Consider yourselves my most

special guests. You'll never have lived more luxuriously.

ME: Thank you. A generous offer.

AVIDITÀ: It's not really an offer.

Again, our silence spoke for us.

"If you'll excuse me," he said, standing, folding his napkin and placing it on the table. "The fall of the Corkscrew has created an enormous amount of work, and there're details to which I must attend. Take your time, enjoy the coffee, order anything you wish."

"Except a ride out of here?" I asked.

"That," he said, "and a few other things. I bid you good morning."

Before we departed his home, I ordered a stiff Bloody Mary. To go.

XXVIII. TOOTH & TALON

Day 262—

WE'LL GET ONE CHANCE.

If we screw it up, we figure, Avidità will definitely be "talking about rats in a cage," and our odds of survival will drop near zero. He'd probably hold the dog hostage.

We consider the transmitters beneath our skin, the CopBots flying their unending grid, and who knows what other surveillances. For now though, other than confining us to San Francisco, Avidità has given us leeway. Not confined to our apartment, not even to the building, we can wander the island edge to edge.

His Big Brother vision cannot be perfect, or the Moribund would never have succeeded. If anything, their terrorism tested the thresholds of Avidità's power, uncovered chinks in his omniscience. The destruction wrought by their attack, too, gives us cover, draws away precious Avidità resources, and improves our odds.

Returning to Golden Gate, we explore the intertidal western edge and its fancy docks. Some of these import goods from other Avidità facilities along the Bay and Central Sea, but imports are not the only things which pass through the permeable barrier at the Pacific edge.

Here there are residents who come and go as they please.

Zeus's realm contains within it a pantheon of lesser gods. Many travel by boat—these yachts double as quasi-military ships, most on hydrofoils, some with fancy engines that process seawater into drinking water.

Or fuel.

We target one vessel in particular. The *Potestatem*.

It's undamaged, wasn't here when the tsunami hit. The mega-waves tore whole arms from the wharf, though, including security gates which control access to the water. Destroyed more than a thousand vessels, too, many which patrolled the archipelago and coast.

At will, the *Potestatem's* elderly owner comes and goes. A half-dozen bodyguards accompany him everywhere. Four more remain on the boat, along with a woman who could be the old man's pet or his pilot. We can't decide which.

The boat's security systems and engine appear to respond only to the owner's biometrics—palm, retinal, and voice, near as we can tell.

Through my binoculars, we observe our quarry, along with the rest of the waterline, park, and city. We are terrible spooks, improvising our spy-craft from every James Bond movie we saw before Blight—keep your eyes on the mark, but don't look like you're keeping your eyes on the mark.

CAILÍN:	This is one of the dumbest ideas I've ever heard.
ME:	It can work.
CAILÍN:	Avidità is a man with drones and robots. He recently burnt a city to the ground. What do you think he can do to us?
ME:	A city is big and sits in one place. Hard to lose track of a city. You can burn it down anytime you like.
CAILÍN:	So?

ME:	A boat is small and the Pacific is gigantic. A mote in the eye of a hurricane. You're sure about this kind of yacht?
CAILÍN:	My old employer had one similar.
ME:	You're sure about the autopilot?
CAILÍN:	All these boats, the ones like this, they've got it.
ME:	It'd take us to Anchorage?
CAILÍN:	Easily.
ME:	We're stealing it.
CAILÍN:	This is one of the dumbest ideas I've ever heard.

It wasn't my idea. It was Raymond's. Make it to the coast, to Anchorage, into Fairbanks. Only now I don't give a shit about Fairbanks. It's the standing forests I'm after, the islands of my row-a-boat dream. The dream doesn't tell me where to go, but the imagery suggests Glacier or Berners or Chilkoot.

Cailín knows the dream too, but the details differ for her. In her version of the dream, I wear red and she wears blue.

Nevermore circles far overhead, lazing above Golden Gate.

Earth is dying, Avidità said.

Equatorial furnaces, the tropics spew carbon dioxide even though human pollution has dropped near zero. Tundra and seabeds fart methane. Lower temperate forests burn. The Hothouse. How could anything ever survive this?

Honestly, maybe Blight was the best thing that ever happened.

Cailín and I bought hotdogs. She doused hers in relish, mustard, pickles, and mayonnaise. We sat by the shore, a thumbnail of sand lapped by high tide. Though muted by the city and the thrum of technology, the park grasses spoke to us. The trees groaned. The water ached. The jellies and red algae rocked in rhythm to the waves. Pigeons thrive in San Francisco, like the rats do, living off human detritus. The cockroaches outnumber everything. Vultures ride the thermals above the Bay. Seagulls scavenge more than pigeons and rats. Dormant locusts bide their time. Out on the Wastes, coyotes make do, and snakes have resurged.

A vulture lands near Cailín and hops to her. She offers it the remainder of her hotdog, which it gobbles. Passersby gave this scene a wide berth.

Teeth and talons. Plenty. Everywhere, if we're patient.

ME: Maybe let the vulture go.
CAILÍN: I suppose you're right.

She shooed it away, and it took flight. In the nearby cottonwoods, the conspiracy of ravens had returned. Dozens, at quick count.

Nevermore roosted above them, preening himself.

XXIX. AUTOPILOT

Day 273—

I'VE BEEN THINKING ABOUT the old man we killed in San Francisco.

Unlike another old man, I learned this one's name.

I've been thinking about the bullet which got Cailín, and dreams of black and white, of red and blue.

Three times, in the days leading up to zero hour, our liaison called us into Avidità's tower. Always blood samples, swabs of our spit, snot into a tissue. I refused their other requests, but Cailín played along better, which made her the wiser. Our freedoms as such depended on cooperation.

We established routines which took us from the building. Without effort, it was possible to live entirely in Avidità's tower. Every need provided. Food, clean water, heat, air-conditioning, exercise, art, music, views, anything. We chalked our excursions down to preference, foremost to an Irish pub where Cailín connected with a handful of Irish boys who, like her, found themselves trapped in the Americas when Blight crescendoed.

Irish boys. Catholic or protestant, didn't matter much, never mind the resurgent power of Rome. Secular boys with the genetic echo of superstitious Celts, whose blood echoed with the raven tales of the Morrígan or the thundering horses of Epona.

What a chaos in the end—

We needed the old man aboard the *Potestatem,* but that meant his bodyguards would be there too. We summoned our forces to match, and it was never going to be clean or easy or clockwork. This wasn't a spy thriller but goddamned desperate people willing to kill or be killed.

Every other option led to rat-in-cage horrors, or to our deaths.

ME:	We negotiate with the yacht's owner.
CAILÍN:	With what? Our charm? Our bodies? We have no special power over men.
ME:	We appeal to his humanity.
CAILÍN:	And if he doesn't have any? He reports us to Avidità, who by the way is actually his peer and King, so again—
ME:	We steal the boat while he's away.
CAILÍN:	Can we find a hacker who can bypass the biometers?
ME:	Maybe—
CAILÍN:	Where do we find this hacker?
ME:	Ask around.
CAILÍN:	Fifty-fifty odds they also report us to Avidità—
ME:	We kidnap the owner. If we take him on land, we'll have six guards to contend with, not ten.
CAILÍN:	Better, but all kinds of things can go awry between "on land" and sailing into the sunset.
ME:	Then we have to take everyone at once. Got any ideas?

Her answers shocked me.

I questioned then her innocence in Prince George, when she denied responsibility for those armless, tongueless, hopeless human weapons the Horned Lords marched into town. I'm thinking of half-truths. I'm thinking of points-of-view.

It exhausted us, gathering our army. An army of feathers, fur, scales, shells, chitin. To summon a rabbit is nothing, but to call bestial squadrons—by the time we boarded the yacht, I was surprised I could stand, as if the command of flying, biting, crawling, jumping things could drain me vampire-like.

A thousand animal corpses on the wharf, on the decks, in the cabins. Tiny birds diced in the rotors of drones, the drones shattered on the docks or submerged in the waters. Ten bodyguards picked by vultures and ravens. The woman we thought a pet or pilot locked herself in a closet and barred the door, screaming at us to leave. Between screams the old man gave the yacht's voice command. He gave Cailín his hand and his eye too.

The Irish boys untied the yacht from the cleats, climbed aboard, and heaved us from shore.

Three minutes passed from first blitz to bloody end.

Avidità's response took less.

Three more drones crashed through a cloud of birds, seagulls drawn through jet engines or rotors. CopBots burned through locust clouds and roach swarms, their motors gummed and shrieking, but not before littering the starboard with bullets. An Irish boy careened overboard, lost, no way to save him even if he survived the fall. By now we raced to ninety knots, insane speeds, the hull rising from the water, the hydrofoils skimming. The engines hummed and the AI bobbed through the waves, a slalom, a dodge-and-weave.

Another Irish boy vomited over the side, but he managed to grip the railing.

The CopBots fell away. Only one drone remained, and by then we'd outraced our own army. Clear of our interference, that drone could launch missiles. It could blow us from the water.

Instead, it disengaged, circled, and retreated.

I will spend months wondering why.

ME:	Cailín, I think we made it!
ME:	Cailín?
ME:	Cailín!
ME:	God, Cailín, this can't be the meaning of my dream.
ME:	Cailín! Don't fucking die.
ME:	Nodens, you asshole!

She still breathed, but a bullet had punched below her collarbone. Her blood mixed with the blood of the many dead, pooling around her. I couldn't tell what was hers and what wasn't. If ever I thought her pale before, now I saw death, now I understood.

Red for power, blue for order, white for mourning, black for—

The pet/pilot banged on the door of her locked closet.

PET/PILOT:	Hey! Hey, you bitch! I can save her!
ME:	What?
PET/PILOT:	I can save her, but you have to promise not to kill me.
ME:	You can save her?
PET/PILOT:	I'm a doctor. I am—or I was—Mr. Strickland's personal physician.

ME: Save her, and you will live a long and
                 blessed life.
DOCTOR: Let me get to work.

I've been thinking about how many assumptions I've
made. I've been thinking I should stop that habit.

XXX. TWO IF BY SEA

Day 291—

By the time we passed forty-five degrees north latitude, the *Potestatem's* AI had steered us two hundred klicks from Oregon's shore. I hoped to glimpse the ruins of Salem, but like my old fantasy of taking revenge for the murders of Phil and Terry, the opportunity slipped away. While on the Pacific we spotted a half dozen other boats, including a luxury cruiser, though none posed any threat to us, pirates or not. In total, our route crossed a thousand nautical miles, thirty hours in our hydrofoil.

Nevermore rode on a platform behind the cabin, protected from the wind.

Our journey brought us past Graham Island and the southernmost tip of Alaska, as far north as Prince George. It'd taken Cailín and I a month to cover the same distance overland, north to south. As we passed into the strait between Baranof Island and Kuiu Island, an Irish boy cancelled the AI's automatic pilot and manually guided us into a labyrinth of forested archipelagos—much more extensive than before Pulse Three, and unmapped, reaching deeply into what used to be Canada. Clouds covered the sky and rain fell steadily.

We settled into cabins, near the water, a vacationers' paradise originally built seventy meters above sea level. One building held a dozen Blighted corpses, now dried husks, and we burned these.

The doctor called herself Jane Falwell. She saved Cailín's life, then made her demands.

JANE:	I don't know what the hell happened yesterday, why it was all like Alfred Hitchcock and his goddamned Birds, or what kind of technology did that. I don't care. But you promised me a "long and blessed life."
ME:	Yes.
JANE:	I'll settle for the hydrofoil. Give it to me. Let me go back to San Francisco.
ME:	Aching to reach orbit?
JANE:	The Stations are real, and they're designed to last generations. You think you're safe here in the north? That it won't warm enough to kill the trees and whatever crops you manage to grow?
ME:	Blight took the pressure off. Must be less than a hundred million humans left, maybe fifty million. The Earth can come back.
JANE:	Of course Blight took the pressure off—it was designed to do that—but the Earth isn't coming back by itself, not for a million years.
ME:	Designed?
JANE:	Blight is a corporate invention.
ME:	You know this?
JANE:	I've been close enough to the inner circles. Runaway climate change isn't stopping because humans are gone. The icecaps aren't coming back. Ocean acidity isn't dropping. Blight was step one in a bigger plan—put the survivors

	in Arks, control the culture of their children, engineer Earth from space, impose an ice age—
ME:	How?
JANE:	Atmospheric manipulation. I don't know those details. I'm a medical doctor, not a geo-engineer. I've heard no one thinks the Earth will be comfortable for another thousand years—optimistic scenario.
ME:	Who thinks this?
JANE:	The C-level folks. Point is, without intervention, even Alaska will see summertimes halfway to boiling point. Your plan to snuggle down and wait for a revival is doomed.
ME:	Let me show you something.

I checked on Cailín. Stable, resting, in good spirits. I'm thinking about how our dreams are imperfect premonitions. During the battle, had the doctor not locked herself away, our army would have torn her to pieces and a CopBot bullet would have taken Cailín's life. The difference between white and black or red and blue turned on a flimsy closet latch and the misidentified staff doctor of a dead trillionaire.

Nodens doesn't show us the future. Even he cannot see that. He is like a chess master looking over the shoulders of two novices, helping us make better moves.

After leaving Cailín, I led Jane into the woods. We sat in a clearing, and I laid my hand against the mossy ground.

JANE: What're we doing?
ME: Shh.

Compared with San Francisco or the Wastes, this ground pulsed with life. Closing my eyes, I found my vision improved. The movements of animals, glimpses of their sight, the scents they followed, the trees which housed them like a chapel, which like ganglia gave the earth its own senses.

A grizzly bear. Wolves. Two mountain lions. They formed a circle around us. Jane managed to stay seated.

JANE: Jesus Christ—
ME: Shh.

Ravens gathered in the trees and cawed. Grasses grew between my fingers, threading between them, growing centimeters a minute. Beside my hand, stalks lengthened and wildflowers bloomed.

ME: I have a different vision for the future
               of this world.
JANE: You could show this to the Corp-
               orations, change everything.
ME: I'm not showing them anything.
JANE: Why not?
ME: Because I'm going to crush them.

The bear escorted us back to the cabins. Jane never again asked to leave, and she's chosen one of the Irish boys for her own. They live in the cabin closet to the water. I would write of everything which she's done to establish a medical network along the coast, connected through Prince George, but I'll save that for another day.

Cailín is twenty-seven weeks along, healthy and well. She and I, too, tried to claim an Irish boy for our own. We infected him, watched the stain take his mouth and lips, wept as he went mad. He grew strong as any beast, short-tempered and violent, lost in dreams of blood.

He died. I can't yet write of that either, but Cailín and I have learned our lesson.

I've been thinking about how barbaric it's all become, this new Dark Ages. It won't be long before we push it back, though there may be much superstition and many human sacrifices. Our society shall be one that cannot forget the lessons of modernity, of industrialization, but which will walk with the Old Gods.

Sometimes at night, out to sea, gigantic forms wade to the horizon.

Last week, in the woods, I glimpsed a silver-haired, lissome woman. She stood three meters, at least, and a horse-sized wolf loped at her side. With only one glance my way, she passed from view, her business her own and no one else's.

Right now, Nevermore sits outside my open window, clicking his beak and cleaning himself. I'm reviewing plans for the circle of standing stones we intend to erect on the adjacent island, but that project will wait for springtime.

The sun has set. Snow is falling and the hush is so deep that I can hear the rush of blood in my ears. When the world ends, I've been thinking, another must always begin.

Isn't that what all the old mythologies say?

ABOUT J.L. FORREST

J.L. Forrest has been a college professor, an international scholar, an expatriate, a medal-winning martial artist, a trophy-winning archer, a ticket-winning Skee Ball player, a wilderness survivalist, a sailor, a corporate consultant, an architect, a horseman, a rock-and-roll guitarist, and an utter layabout. All this amounted to nothing more than preparation for the real challenge—

Writing.

Scrawlings of science fiction and dark fantasy.

Literary musings and whatever else drip from his pen.

He is the award-winning author of dozens of short stories, which have appeared in the likes of *Analog Science Fiction and Fact,* Crossed Genres, Third Flatiron, Robot Cowgirl Press, and others. An active member of the Science Fiction and Fantasy Writers of America, J.L. Forrest is also an advocate for literacy, literature, and literary shenanigans of most kinds.

For more than a decade, he has made his primary home in Colorado, but occasionally finds himself ensconced in the Pacific Northwest or in the Old Country of Italia.

In bocca al lupo!

MORE READING

REQUIES DAWN — A novel of the far future

Short-story collections

DELICATE MINISTRATIONS

MINUSCULE TRUTHS

For special offers and new releases, join the mailing list at:

http://jlforrest.com/newsletter/

Or learn more at:

http://jlforrest.com/

Be sure to listen to the track, "When the World Ends":

https://nicefm.bandcamp.com/album/when-the-world-ends-deluxe-single-novella

If you liked this story, the best things you can do for the author are **recommend J.L. Forrest's books to others** and **leave a positive review on Amazon**.

CPSIA information can be obtained
at www.ICGtesting.com
Printed in the USA
LVHW11s1609210918
590921LV00001B/28/P

9 780998 949291